# Bella at Midnight

# Bella at Midnight

# Bella
## *at*
# Midnight

## DIANE STANLEY

*Illustrated by*
## BAGRAM IBATOULLINE

HARPERCOLLINS*PUBLISHERS*

Library of Congress Cataloging-in-Publication Data

Stanley, Diane.

Bella at midnight / Diane Stanley ; illustrated by Bagram Ibatoulline.—1st ed.

p. cm.

Summary: Raised by peasants, Bella discovers that she is actually the daughter of a knight and finds herself caught up in a terrible plot that will change her life and the kingdom forever.

ISBN-10: 0-06-077573-4—ISBN-10: 0-06-077574-2 (lib. bdg.)

ISBN-13: 978-0-06-077573-5—ISBN-13: 978-0-06-077574-2 (lib. bdg.)

[1. Knights and knighthood—Fiction. 2. Princes—Fiction. 3. Kings, queens, rulers, etc.—Fiction. 4. Sex role—Fiction.] I. Ibatoulline, Bagram, ill. II. Title.

PZ7.S7869Bel 2006    2005005906

[Fic]—dc22

Typography by Amy Ryan

4  5  6  7  8  9  10

First Edition

For Martha,
and for Jim—
who introduced me to
Kitty-Pair-of-Kitties
and the king of the fairies

# Bella at Midnight

# BOOK ONE

## *The Thimble*

# MAUD

When the message came and I saw it was from Edward, I nearly choked on my plum cake. It could only mean that my sister was dead.

I had not seen her since her wedding day, three long years before. An occasion for rejoicing—that's what you're imagining, is it not? A beautiful bride, a blushing groom, flowers, and music, and bright new beginnings?

It's a sweet picture, but that is not how it was, not for Catherine, anyway. Oh, she *did* look a perfect angel in her delicate gown of robin's-egg blue, her hair cascading down her shoulders, shining like the finest gold. And there *were* flowers aplenty, and music, too, and a sumptuous feast that lasted well into the night. Father wanted nothing but the best for her, you see. But as for the bright new beginnings—well, that's another story. You'll notice I haven't yet mentioned the groom.

Sir Edward of Burning Wood was an odd man, arrogant and proud. But I thought such traits to be common among the nobility. I knew little of such things, being born to the merchant class. And so I would have taken his peculiar and unfriendly ways as natural to his station in life—if it hadn't been for the way he looked at me. There was such coldness in those eyes, such a hardness near to hatred, that it positively made me tremble, and I could not help but turn away. I remember thinking, when first he pierced me with that terrible gaze, that Edward of Burning Wood was not altogether right in his mind.

He was no proper husband for my sister, of that I was sure—and I told Father so.

"Catherine is rich," I said, "and beautiful besides— she does not need to settle for such a man."

"*Settle?*" Father said. He was astonished, for he considered it a splendid match. "What can you be thinking? Edward is a knight, and he shall make our Catherine a lady. Just think of it, Maud—and she only a glass merchant's daughter!"

"A glass merchant's daughter with a *fortune*,

Father, don't forget that." (I knew, and Father knew, and surely even Catherine knew that Edward was marrying her for her money.) "I would far rather she remain a common lass than be raised to the nobility and be miserable all her life!"

"But why should she be miserable?" Father countered. "Can you not see how the man dotes upon her?"

This was true enough; Edward did seem besotted with my sister, for all that he wed her for gain. Yet even in this he was extreme and unnatural—for his was a wild, possessive, fanatical love. Catherine was flattered by it, of course. Moreover, she thought him handsome and admired his confidence and manly bearing.

And so, as both Father and Catherine seemed so pleased with the arrangement, I resolved to keep my doubts to myself and say no more against the man.

After the wedding—indeed, the very next day—it became clear that I had greatly underestimated Edward: he was far, far worse than even *I* had believed him to be! For once he was in possession of both Catherine and her dowry, he turned his back on us, forbidding my sister to ever see us again!

Can you imagine such a thing? Why, it nearly put poor Father in his grave. Indeed, it was at about that time that his mind began to wander and he became childlike in his ways, as the old are sometimes wont to do. But I believe it was the loss of Catherine that caused him to decline—that and the guilt he felt over giving her in marriage to such a terrible man.

And perhaps his infirmity was a blessing of sorts, for as I opened Edward's letter now, I took some small comfort from the knowledge that, however dreadful its contents might be, Father was past suffering over it anymore.

I scanned the message quickly, searching it for words such as *dead* or *death*—but they were nowhere in evidence. I am a poor reader, I confess, and tears blurred my sight. Also, Edward's script was cramped and small and difficult to make out. But I struggled through it, word by word, until at last I reached the heart of the letter and—what joy!—discovered that my sister was *not* dead, not in the least! She was about to give birth to her first child—and I had not even known she was expecting!

I squinted now, concentrating hard in my eagerness to learn what more the letter might tell me. I could not imagine that Edward had written me out of courtesy, even at such a time. And of course I was right; he wanted something. He wanted me to go there—to that house he had bought with my father's money, to which we had never once been invited—he wanted me to go there and comfort dear Catherine in her labor! He said he did not like the looks of the midwife.

He is afraid, I thought, afraid for Catherine's life—for indeed, she was always a delicate creature and had never been strong. Now he feared to lose her, and he was so desperate that he had even stooped to asking *me* for help.

Well. I would do it for Catherine. I would gladly suffer his haughty pride and sharp tongue for *her* sake. And a new babe—oh, how the prospect stirred my spirit! I would go at once!

And so I wrapped up well against the cold, roused the kitchen maid, and bid her keep an eye on Father (lest he wake in the darkness and, in his confusion, miss the chamber pot again). Then I rode off with the messenger in the direction of my sister's house. It was full dark by the time I got there. As I mounted the steps, I heard the bells ring for Compline. The monks would be going to prayer and then to bed. But I knew there would be no rest for me that night.

Edward let me in himself. His looks alarmed me, so pale and wild eyed did he appear. Things must be very bad indeed, I thought. But he said nothing, only turned and led me to the chamber wherein Catherine lay. There he left me. Childbirth is women's business; there was naught for him to do but wait out in the hall, pacing and grumbling. Catherine was in God's hands now—and in the midwife's, and in mine.

I went inside and closed the door. It was dark in that great, cold room, for all the candles that were burning. Yet I could see my sister well enough, her dear face damp with sweat, her cheeks bright, and her arms outstretched to embrace me. Oh, we were a pair, my sister and I, weeping and laughing and clinging to each other like two mad things!

"Oh, Maud," she whispered through her tears, "I am safe now that you are here. I shall not die, I am sure of it! For you have God's healing touch—you always did!"

"Nonsense," I said, kissing her forehead and stroking her hands as tenderly as though she were a child. "*Of course* you shall be well, silly girl. And soon you shall be a mother, too, of a fine fat babe. Now won't that be grand?"

She squeezed my hand in answer, and kissed it, then closed her eyes. She had been in labor some hours already, and it had worn her out.

All this time the midwife had been busily rummaging about in her bag of potions and charms, as though looking for something. But I think it was only her way of giving us a bit of privacy for our reunion, for she now abandoned her search and returned to the bedside.

"Well, then, my lady," she said, "you must be the dear girl's sister!"

"Indeed I am," I replied—though I need not have bothered, for she was not listening. She continued to chatter away, unceasingly, until I began to think she was driven to it by demons! Truly, she scarcely paused to draw breath. And what an endless, mindless, pointless, unbearable monologue it was, too! I was sorely tempted to strike her upon the head with the fire tongs, just to make her stop!

Not until she had discussed the weather (it was uncommonly cold), her health (she had a terrible aching in the joints), Edward's house (it was ever so grand), and her journey there (she had lost her way; she had encountered beggars at the crossroads, filthy creatures who did not deserve one penny of her hard-earned money; she had twisted her ankle and fallen into the gutter and fouled her skirt most horribly), did she finally arrive at the subject of my sister's health. Though this was at least appropriate to the occasion, it proved to be even more intolerable.

"Now you need not fret, my lady," she said with uncalled-for cheeriness while rubbing some oily, foul-smelling paste onto Catherine's swollen belly. "The babe is well presented, headfirst, just as we like it to be—because when they are turned around the other way, you see, feetfirst—well, that's bad. And sometimes they get wrapped up in the cord, poor little things, all strangled like. You are sure to lose the babe when that happens, and sometimes the mother, too, and there is naught anybody can do about it. But there's no sign of any of that here, my lady. No, no— not to worry! No need to worry at all. It just takes time—oh, my, yes! A good many hours with the first one—sometimes days! Why, there was this one poor lady who was in labor for nigh on a week, and—"

*"Please!"* I cried. "Stop it! I will not hear another word!"

My rebuke appeared to astonish her, for her face went red with embarrassment and indignation. Still, she managed to hold her tongue after that (though sullenly) for a little while, at least. And a blessed relief it was, too.

Time passed slowly; it seemed an age before the matins bell chimed the midnight hour.

"A new day," I said to Catherine, wiping her brow with a damp cloth.

"A new year!" added the midwife, who had recovered her spirits by then and was back to talking.

"So it is," I agreed with a sigh. "I had forgot it."

"And no common one, neither," she said. "It marks a hundred years since we first went to war with Brutanna!"

"Aye," I said. "I had forgot that, too. Not a thing to celebrate, though."

"Oh, well, now, some say different! And if you

think about it, my lady—a *hundred* years! Now that's *significant*, if you know what I mean. People say that God will send us a miracle now and bring the war to an end! There have been signs and portents!"

"What sort of signs?"

"Well, there was a farmer grew a turnip, looked exactly like the Blessed Virgin! That's one. And a calf off in Chesney was born with two heads!"

"Foolishness," I said. "Freaks of nature."

"Oh, no, my lady—they're signs! Everybody says so. There's going to be a great miracle. Surely you have heard the prophecy—it is on every tongue!"

"No," I muttered, "I have not heard it."

"Indeed! How very strange! Well, I shall tell you then. It is about the Worthy Knight—a great hero, you see, pure of heart and most virtuous. One day soon he will appear upon the battlefield, all of a sudden—in armor the color of snow. And instead of a helmet, they say, he will wear a halo of heavenly fire!" Here she demonstrated by waving her none-too-clean hands about her head while wiggling her fingers (presumably to suggest the flickering of flames). "And he won't carry a sword or a lance, neither, but *only the banner of peace*!" She raised her right arm and waved an imaginary banner. "And at the sight of him, all the soldiers will fall upon their knees and lay their weapons down. And *that* will be the end of the war!"

"Well," I said, making the sign of the cross. "It is a pretty tale. God grant that it may be so. We could use a hero in these times." And I meant it kindly, too, for all that the woman annoyed me. It was common folk such as her who suffered most of the death and destruction in wartime. No wonder they turned to superstition and miraculous stories.

Catherine cried out as another labor pain seized her.

"Merciful Lord," I muttered, "will this never be over?"

"In good time, madam. In good time," the midwife said, as though speaking to an impatient child. "All the same, it might be well to take out the pins from your sister's hair and let it lie free upon the pillow. Perhaps that will loosen things up a bit. And while you're at it, unplait your own hair, also."

I did as she instructed and untied all the knots I could find. Then we called the housemaid and sent her out to open all the drawers and cupboards in the house. And, God be praised, just a few hours later, as first dawn began to light the room and I was putting out the candles, Catherine was delivered safely of a baby girl.

I fell upon my knees and thanked Our Heavenly Father for bringing my sister through her hour of peril. Then I bathed the child myself with salt and warmed water, wiped her dry, and rubbed her all over with rose oil till she glowed a healthy pink and was as fragrant as a summer bouquet. I put a dollop of honey into her mouth so that she would nurse heartily and grow strong. Then I wrapped her tight in clean linen, which sweet Catherine had embroidered along the hem with tiny blossoms, and carried her out to Edward.

"Catherine is well," I told him joyfully, "and here is your new daughter."

As you might expect, he was sore disappointed that she was not a boy. Indeed, he scarcely even looked at her. But he was most grateful that his wife had survived her ordeal and went in to her straight-away.

That night Catherine developed a fever. A physician was called, and he bled her and gave her some powders. But neither seemed to do her any good—in truth, she seemed somewhat weaker after his visit than she was before. Edward stayed at her side all that night and would not let me near her.

I roused the cook and bid her warm some cow's milk over the fire. Then I took a clean cloth and soaked a corner of it in the milk and touched it to the baby's lips. At first she turned her face away angrily, but she was so hungry that soon she was sucking at it mightily.

"In the morning you must find a wet nurse for the child," the cook said.

"That is Sir Edward's prerogative, not mine," I answered, dipping the rag in the warm milk again. "He would not like for me to interfere in a matter of such importance — though I suppose, things being as they are, it would not hurt to find someone to fill in, just for a while."

And so the following day, I asked around and was directed pretty quickly to a butcher's wife who had just buried a child and still had plenty of milk. She agreed to come and nurse our little babe until my sister was better and a permanent choice could be made.

But the next day Catherine was worse. I could not bear that Edward kept me away, for I know I could have comforted her. At the very least I might have told her good-bye and laid the child in her arms one last time.

But he barred the door and stayed in there three long days. He would not allow Cook to bring in food. He would not even answer when we pounded upon the door. Only on the fourth day did he come out. Catherine had been dead all that time. It was well that it was winter, for had the room been warm, her body would have begun to stink. I do not think I could have borne it.

Throughout that dark time, the child was never mentioned and little thought of, except by me. It was only after the funeral that I dared speak of her at all.

"Edward," I said, "I know it is hard to think of such things when we are all so brokenhearted—but should we not gather the godparents now and take the babe to the priest to be christened?"

"Just take her away," he said.

"I will carry her home with me, then, if you like. I would be right glad to do that."

He rose to his feet of a sudden and strode over to where I stood with my back against the wall. He leaned down over me and breathed into my face. His expression was so wild, his eyes so piercing, I feared he might do me harm. But he only hissed—and I could feel drops of spittle upon my face as he spoke— "If I like? If I like? I would *like* you to *get her out of here*! I do not want that creature in this house, do you understand? Nor in *your* house, nor anywhere in this city! I will not breathe the same air she breathes!"

"Oh, Edward," I stammered, "you must at least take her to the priest! You are obliged to do that much, surely—to look after her immortal soul!"

*"Get out!"* he screamed.

And so I fled the room, my heart pounding, and hurried to the kitchen where Cook was minding the child. I gathered the wee thing in my arms and ran from that house as though fleeing from the devil.

I took her to the priest myself that very day and had her christened. I named her Isabel, after my mother, who is with the angels.

The next morning, accompanied by the butcher's wife, we set out with a small mule train in the direction of Burning Wood, Edward's country estate. It stands near to Castle Down, the great seat of the duke of Claren. And it was in the duke's village that I found a home for Isabel—in the house of a blacksmith by the name of Martin.

His wife, Beatrice, was a sensible woman, kindhearted and clean. I liked her immensely, right from the start. And moreover, she was so well thought of in those parts that she had lately served as wet nurse to a *royal prince*!

Yes, I thought, this woman would do excellently well! And so it was with an easy mind that I left the child there, in that tidy little cottage, and returned home the next day.

# BEATRICE

Is it not curious how noble folk are so eager to be rid of their children? I have seen it myself, for I have nursed two of their babes, one right after the other. Both of them came from the King's City—halfway across the country—and straight from the lying-in chamber, too!

Oh, I understand that great ladies do not nurse their own infants, any more than they wash them or dress them or change their dirty linen. And in the case of Isabel, of course, the poor mother was dead. But would you not think that the father, having lost his wife, would wish to keep his child close by, so that he might look in on her now and again, and take comfort from the sight of her? Surely there are nursemaids enough in the King's City.

But I ought not to judge my betters. They are highborn folk and educated, so if they think it wise to send their little ones away and leave them in the care of strangers, then I suppose it must be the right thing to do. And indeed, now that I think upon it, if those two precious babes had been kept at home, then Prince Julian and Isabel would never have met, and all the great and miraculous things that happened thereafter would not have taken place. I do not claim to understand such things, whether it was the wisdom of great folk or the hand of God that caused those events to unfold as they did. But surely all in the kingdom should be grateful for it.

Nineteen years ago, it was, that one of the ladies from the duke's household came to ask me to serve as nursemaid to little Prince Julian, the king's youngest babe. It seems the queen was not overly fond of rowdy boys always disturbing her peace and overturning the furniture. She already had three young princes running about the palace; four was one too many. And as the king's brother, the duke of Claren, had agreed to foster Julian and train him up to knighthood, the queen decided to send him to Castle Down straightaway, and not wait till he was seven, as is the common practice. That is why they were in need of a wet nurse, you see, here in the duke's village.

I told them I would be honored to serve the little prince, but I did not wish to go up and live at the castle. I had my own boy, Will, to look after, and my husband, Martin, too.

"It does not matter," the lady said. "You may keep him here till he is weaned."

Now this was another mystery: that they should allow a royal prince to live with the likes of *me*—a common peasant they would not suffer to sit down beside them at their own table! As if caring for their children and scrubbing their floors were much the same sort of thing!

Of course they *did* provide for the prince as was fitting—sending him all manner of embroidered blankets and lace-trimmed smocks and dear little bonnets to shade his eyes from the sun. And when he was old enough to eat a bit of porridge, he ate it from a silver dish with a silver spoon—but he ate it in a peasant cottage all the same.

Once he was weaned, Julian was taken back to Castle Down, where the women of the duke's household would see to his care. He cried when the ladies came for him, and no wonder—I was the only mother he had ever known. Yet they scolded him for weeping and called him an unmanly fellow—and he only three years old! It like to broke my heart!

We stood there in the yard, my boy, Will, and me, and watched as they carried our little prince up the lane toward the castle. I never will forget it, Julian looking back at us over the lady's shoulder, wailing and reaching out his little hand to bid us good-bye. There was naught we could do but wave back at him and throw kisses—oh, but it was dreadful sad!

I think God must have looked down upon us then and seen how lonely and dejected we were without our little prince. And so, not three days later, He sent a little princess to take his place.

She was not really a princess—we only called her that—but she was highborn, the daughter of a knight. Her aunt brought her to us, saying the babe had lost its mother and was in need of a nursemaid. The cook up at Burning Wood had spoken well of me, saying I had lately served as wet nurse to the king's youngest son. That was the reason they came to me, I am sure of it. For whenever gentlefolk hear you had aught to do with royalty, they think you grander than you really are—as if Julian's greatness had rubbed off on me as I suckled him and changed his dirty linen! I suppose the aunt figured that if I was good enough for a prince, I was good enough for Isabel.

Like Julian, she came from the King's City. The father had sent her here so that she might "enjoy the benefits of country life." At least that's what the auntie said, though I was sure there was more to that story than what she was telling; I could see it in her face. But it mattered not to me. Our house felt empty with Julian gone. And as we could use the money, and as the sweet babe needed the milk I could provide, we took her in. We never dreamed how long she would stay.

# BEATRICE

*I*sabel had not been with us a week when Julian came to visit for the first time. He had wept and screamed so, poor thing, that one of the ladies—to preserve her sanity, she said—agreed to carry him down to the village. After that she brought him often, for she said the prince was always easier to manage after he had been at our house. Later, of course, he came to us on his own, two or three times in a week. It was not far—only five minutes from the castle gate to our door.

When Julian first saw Isabel, I believe he thought she was some new toy we had brought in especially for his amusement! He begged me to unwrap her so that he could see how tiny her toes were, and laughed himself into hiccups when she gripped his finger in her little fist and tried to put it in her mouth.

Still a baby himself, Julian could not rightly say "Isabel." He called her "Bel," and later "Bella." So Bella she became, Princess Bella. All the village called her that.

Each time Julian came, he seemed astonished by how she had grown. I know not whether he thought she would stay a babe forever, but he was wild with excitement when she learned to sit up, and later when she took her first steps. Before long they were scampering off together, hand in hand, to play out on the common or down by the river, or to sit upon the wall telling stories and blowing upon grass blades to make the sound of a trumpet.

Seeing the two of them together, you would have thought they were brother and sister. I do not mean that they looked alike—Julian was small and dark and solemn, while Bella was a wild little fairy child with pale-blue eyes and red-gold curls. Yet there was something so like in their natures, some powerful force that bound them together, beyond all explaining. Whatever it was, any fool could see that it was not Martin or Will or me that Julian came to see so often—it was Bella.

At one point he took to calling her the "mistress of

his heart." The other little pages up at the castle had all chosen some girl from the duke's court to honor in this way, and so Julian chose Bella and promised to carry her handkerchief in all his tournaments. He was far too young for such things, of course—I daresay he was only just learning to ride a horse! But they, both of them, liked to pretend, and their little game seemed innocent enough. I never dreamed aught would come of it. Indeed, I do not think *anyone* could have guessed the true consequence of that childish affection.

I only knew that I had been called upon to look after two unwanted children, to give them mother love and start them on their way. Just as in the garden, we dig the earth and scatter the seed and give water to the tender plants—but it is God who makes them grow. I did all I could for those little ones—and looking back, I see it was enough. God had His own great business afoot. I just played my small part in it. And when all was revealed, well, I marveled as much as anyone.

# WILL

My parents thought we were asleep. And indeed, Bella was—but I lay awake, listening as they talked in quiet voices up in the loft. They did not know how the sound carried in the stillness.

Mother had often told me it is ill-mannered to listen to others in secret. But I needed to hear what she would say to Father about the steward's visit, and what it might signify for Bella, and for us.

It had happened in the morning, while I was out weeding the garden. Bella was not allowed to help, for she was only three and could not yet tell the weeds from the sallet herbs. And so she sat beside me in the dirt, asking her everlasting questions.

"Is *that* a weed? Is *that* a weed?" she asked me many times.

"Why do you *hate* the weeds? Does it *hurt* them when you pull them out? Are they *dead* now?"

To me the weeds were just a nuisance and a chore; to Bella they were living out some great tragic story! I never knew if it was her fine breeding that made her so fanciful, or if she was just touched in the head, but that child was ever a mystery to me. Once I saw her shaking a little tree with all her might, and when I asked her what she was about, she said, "I am making the wind blow!" How could you not love a creature like that?

I was about to send her into the house to fetch my hat—as much to stop the questions as to spare my head from the sun—when I looked up and saw the steward riding down the road in our direction. He worked for Bella's father, and he came over from the estate at Burning Wood every quarter to pay Mother's wages.

I had just been thinking of late how much Bella had grown, and that the steward was sure to come for her soon, just as the duke's ladies had come for Julian. So when I saw him riding toward the cottage, my chest went tight. I did not want Bella to go.

But the steward did not seem to notice her when

he rode into the yard. He only asked where Mother might be. I said I would run fetch her from the back of the house, where she was doing the washing. I picked Bella up and carried her with me. I did not like to leave her there with the steward.

Mother dried her hands upon her apron and brushed off her skirts to look as presentable as might be. I saw from her face that she thought the same as I did—that he had come to take Bella away. She touched the child's curls most tenderly; then we walked together round the side of the house.

"Your wages," the steward said, handing her a small purse of coins, just as he always did. That done, he turned to ride off again. We looked at each other in surprise. This was not what we had expected.

"Steward," Mother called after him. "Please wait a moment! I must know what arrangements have been made for this child."

I do not think it was easy for my mother to speak so boldly to such a man. He looked back at her in that haughty way important people do.

"She has been fostered on *you*, lady. *That* is the arrangement."

"But sire, she has been weaned these past two months now and is growing fast. Should she not return to her father's house, to be raised up properly as a gentlewoman?"

"I have been given no such instructions," said he crossly. "I am to pay your wages—that is all I know." Then he rode away. Mother stood in the road for some long while, gazing after him with her mouth agape.

What did it mean, I wondered. That Bella would stay with us for always? That her father did not want her? Had he given his child away to us?

I was still holding her. She had wrapped her little arms around my neck and leaned her head upon my shoulder. Her damp curls tickled my cheek. She did not know something important had just happened.

"Mother?" I said. But she only touched my arm and walked away, shaking her head. She was greatly troubled, I could tell that much. But she said nothing more of the matter that day, nor did she mention it to Father when he came home from the forge. I think she did not wish Bella to hear what she had to say. That is why she waited until night to speak of it, when she thought we were asleep.

"I cannot understand," I heard her say, "how he could abandon his child in this way and make no sort of proper arrangements for her!"

"Aye," Father said, "though methinks there must be some reason for it. We cannot know the circumstances, Bea. As he is a knight, like as not he has gone to fight in the war."

"Then he ought to send her to live with his family, if he must go to war—or with the nuns."

"True enough. He chose instead to impose upon us. And by my troth, it galls me that he did not think to *ask* whether we were willing to raise his child or no."

"Are you not, Martin?"

"You know I am, Bea. But he might have *asked*."

They were quiet, then, for a time. I rose up on one elbow and looked over where Bella lay, on her pallet by the fire. Little children in their sleep are nice to look upon, as everybody knows. And Bella, so noisy and active when awake, was all the more sweet at rest. Her breathing was soft and even, her expression innocent and trusting.

It was not right, I thought, for a child to be shifted about like a sack of barley—dropped upon our doorstep and abandoned there, argued over by my parents, as though they did not want her either. *Someone* ought to cherish her.

"What if he never sends for her?" Mother asked after a while. "What am I to do then? I do not know how to raise a knight's child!"

"Rubbish! Of course you do—look at our Will! Is he not as fine a boy as any in the village?"

"Oh, Martin, you know that is not the same! Will is common born, like us. But Bella is of noble estate and must be raised up to live the life she was born to. And I cannot do that—I am ignorant of her world. I cannot even write my name! A crow cannot raise a nightingale!"

"No one expects you to train her in the lady arts, Bea. But you can teach her to work hard—same as you taught Will—and to say her prayers and to be kind and to respect her elders and suchlike. You can teach her to do the right things in life."

"True enough," Mother said. "I can do that much."

"Aye, and far better than her father could, I'll warrant—as he does not seem to know *himself* what is right and needful. All the same, he may remember he has a daughter one day and send for her." Then after a long pause he said, "Until then, well—we have our own little princess."

"Aye," Mother said, "I suppose we do. Though how we are to explain it to the child, I cannot think."

"Oh, we'll find a way when the time comes, when she is older," Father said. "For now we'll just let her be."

I lay back on my pallet and closed my eyes, trying to imagine how that conversation would go. But I could not think of any nice way to tell her the truth: that she had been cast off, unwanted by her father. That the family she thought she belonged to was not truly hers. That they were only the people she was left with, and that they were being *paid* to look after her.

No, it did not bear telling — and the passage of time would not make it any easier. I am sure my parents thought they would explain it to her one day. But that night, young though I was, I knew they never would.

# BELLA

My first memory is of war.

It was late summer, near to harvesttime, and it was hot. I was sprawled in the dust of the yard, playing with a kitten. I had a little twig and was drawing it along the ground so that the kitten would chase after it and pounce upon it. Will had showed me how to do this. "That's how they learn to catch mice," he'd said. I thought it very droll how the kitten would follow wherever I led him.

I was much absorbed in this game when I began to hear shouting from the cottages nearby and then the startling sound of the church bell, ringing the alarm—*clang! clang! clang! clang!* I put my hands over my ears.

Around me the whole village seemed to fly into action, and there was such a lot of noise, with the bells and the screaming and the barking of dogs! I saw men sprinting away toward the upper pasture to drive in the sheep. Mama came running into the yard, telling me to stay where I was, her voice uncommonly hard. I thought she was angry with me, and so I sat there, whimpering and clutching my kitten, while Mama ran about calling for Will to come in from the garden and pulling things off the shelf and putting them into a sack. Then she got baby Margaret out of her cradle, took firm hold of my hand, and told me—in that stern voice again—to stop crying. Soldiers were coming, she said. We must make haste.

I had a little poppet that Mama had made for me out of rags, and I was very fond of her because her cross-stitched eyes were blue, like mine, and her yarn hair was like to my color, which is reddish gold. And I remember asking Mama to go get the poppet, which I had left in the cottage somewhere, but she said we had not the time to look for it.

We joined the stream of people and animals making their way toward the great entrance to the castle. A few men rode horseback; others pulled handcarts piled high with household goods—even small pieces of furniture—not to mention blankets and pots and hams and farm implements and all such things as were deemed precious.

I don't know how old I was then—four or five, I would guess. I know I was small, and all I could see were the legs of people and animals. Everyone was pushing. I grew terrified that the crowd would crush me, and so I started screaming for Mama to pick me up. She couldn't, of course—she had Margaret to carry, and the sack of food—so she just held on to me tighter. I had the kitten in my other hand, and it was trying to get away. I was very unhappy.

"I'll take her, Mama," Will said. He grabbed me around the waist and swung me up onto his back to "ride horse" as he sometimes did at home. It was at that moment—as I grabbed Will's shoulders to keep from falling—that I dropped the kitten!

I screamed and screamed, but the crowd kept surging forward. There was no going back, and my heart just burst open with pain! I wailed with all the force in my little body until a man behind us whacked me across the backside and ordered me to "stop that noise!"

No one had ever struck me before, and I was stunned.

Just then there were shouts of "to the right, to the right," and the crowd grew even more compressed— solid bodies, we were, and sliding sideways. Ahead I could see the cause of it: the duke's men were riding out. A long file of knights and foot soldiers streamed from the castle, ready to take on the raiding party. The villagers cheered.

Once inside the castle walls, Mama found us a place in the courtyard, crowded already with people and their animals and belongings. We would sleep that night in the great hall, but as the day was fine, we stayed outdoors till dark. Papa was busy helping with the sheep.

Prince Julian came looking for us shortly after we arrived. He was dressed splendidly in black and gold, with the royal coat of arms upon his tunic and a real sword at his belt. He was seven or eight, I suppose, and smitten with war fever. He told us breathlessly how he had strapped on his cousin's spurs and helped him don his armor. Then he saw that I had been crying.

"What's the matter with Bella?"

I hid my face in Mama's lap and would not look at him.

"She lost her kitten in the crowd," Mama said, stroking my hair. "Poor wee thing! Then Robert Miller slapped her when she cried."

Hearing her speak of it, I wailed even louder. I wept because the soldiers were coming. I wept because we had been forced from our home and had left my poppet behind. And I wept because the miller had hurt me. But most of all, I wept because I had lost my kitten—and it had been *my fault*! I had not understood that I had to protect it; I had not understood that it could die! And so, because I had been careless, that soft, living creature, which only moments before had been playing so charmingly in our yard, was now crushed and ruined! And no one—*no one*—had the power to bring it back! Oh, how it frightened me, that terrible first experience of guilt and death!

Julian sat down beside me and took me onto his lap. "Hush, Princess Bella," he whispered, "and I will tell you a story about your kitten." I nestled into his embrace and began to feel safe again.

My kitten was a twin, Julian explained, so he was known as "Kitty-Pair-of-Kitties." His brother was always good. He never bit or scratched. He caught lots of mice but always disposed of them properly. He had no fleas and kept his whiskers clean. He was, in other words, of no interest whatsoever.

Kitty-Pair-of-Kitties was just the opposite. He was a perfect rascal and had one hair-raising adventure after another. One day, when he was still only a tiny kitten, he was accidentally dropped into a crowd of people hurrying into a castle. But he was quick on his paws, our hero! The moment he landed, he leaped nimbly onto the back of an ugly man (who was in the habit of smacking poor, innocent little girls) and dug his claws deep into the man's back so that he shrieked like a demon and flung Kitty-Pair-of-Kitties into the bushes, where he landed safely.

Then, as he was hungry and as he thought it likely that someone (being in a hurry) might have left some cream in a butter churn, he hurried off to investigate. Naturally he found one straightaway. He took a flying leap from a windowsill and knocked over the churn, making a terrible mess all over the floor. But being a perfect rascal, Kitty-Pair-of-Kitties didn't care. He just crawled inside, covering himself from head to toe in thick, delicious cream, then proceeded to lick off every bit of it.

After a while he decided it might be well to escape before his crime was detected, so he went trundling out of the house—though not very gracefully, since his tummy had grown so fat and round by then, from eating all that cream, that he could barely walk. Alas, this particular house was at the top of a rise, and Kitty-Pair-of-Kitties lost his balance. Before he could say "meow!" he had rolled tummy over tail all the way to the bottom of the hill!

That seemed as good a place as any to curl up and take a nap. So that's exactly what he did.

"What will he do when he wakes up?" I asked, calmer now.

"He will go help my uncle's knights fight the bad soldiers from Brutanna!"

"How will he do that?"

"Well—I must think. Wait, I know! He will jump

down at them from a tree, and he will land on top of their helmets and peer in through the visors—upside down, you see, like this—and hiss at them!" He demonstrated and made me laugh. "And the soldiers will be so astonished, they will scream and fall off their horses."

"And run away!"

"Yes."

"And will they make him a knight—Kitty-Pair-of-Kitties?"

"Yes, of course they will."

"Good," I said.

That night the sky glowed red, and we smelled smoke in the air. One of the duke's men, who had been standing watch on the ramparts, told us the raiders had torched the village of Seddington, some miles away to the east. "But the duke'll send 'em packing soon enough," the man said.

"That may be," grumbled Thomas, one of our neighbors. "But while the duke is busy fighting over yonder, who's to stop some *more* of 'em from coming over here? They're not addlebrained, you know! They'd like nothing better than to set fire to our fields and burn our village, just to deprive the duke of the income."

Thomas was a sour man, always arguing and stirring up trouble, and so he was called "Thomas the Quarreler," to distinguish him from Thomas Baker.

"Then may God protect us," Papa said.

"As He protected the good folk of Seddington?" Thomas snapped. "Truly, Martin, I do not think God has taken any notice of us these last hundred years and more."

"For shame, Tom!" Mama said. "God *always* watches over us!"

"Perhaps you are right, Beatrice," he said. "Only, would you not think, as He looks down from heaven, that God would begin to grow *weary* of so much death and destruction? Raise a hand to help us down here? Might this not be a good time for that great miracle of His we've been hearing so much about these last few years—the Worthy Knight, who will appear on the field of battle all aglow with heavenly fire, and bring an end to the war? Where *is* he, Beatrice? He is long overdue, don't you think?"

"He may come this very night, Tom, or the next. He will come when God sends him."

"Nonsense," he grumbled. "God is asleep!"

"Thomas!" Papa said. "Mind your tongue! It is a sin to speak thus, and you will bring God's punishment upon us."

"God has *already* punished us," Thomas said. Then he turned away and said no more.

It was late and had been full dark for some time. The duke's servants had lit the torches several hours before. Now, as I lay upon my bed of rushes on the floor, nestled close to Mama, I gazed up at the cavernous space of the great hall, with its giant beams touched by the warm glow of the torchlight. I turned to look at the marvelous tapestry that hung above us, with pictures of hunters and animals and trees upon it, only I could no longer see them in the dim light. And then my eyelids grew heavy and my body softened, and I no longer listened to the conversation of the grown-ups. I was young and I was tired, and so I slept.

I woke while it was still dark. All about me people were moaning and weeping, and I heard angry voices saying "all gone" and "everything" and "may the devil take them." Over and over I heard the word *Brutanna*, spoken like a curse, like a bad taste you spit out of your mouth.

The air reeked of smoke and other foul smells I could not name. I began to cough and wipe my eyes.

"Mama?" I said. But she just patted my hair and said to go back to sleep. Her voice was husky and strange, as though she had been crying.

And then it was morning, and the duke's men had returned. There was not so much smoke anymore, but the smell was still in the air—it would not entirely go away for many months.

I remember little after that—only a few terrible images. But each of them is clear and vivid and distinct in my memory, like the scenes I saw depicted on the great tapestries up at the castle.

I see the smoldering ruins of our village: the network of roads and lanes still there, but where cottages had once stood, only piles of charred beams.

I remember the stinking, blackened fields and poor Mad Walter, all coated with ash, combing the stubble in search of something to eat.

I remember a man, lying in one of the lanes, still as a stone and covered in blood. Mama pulled me away from the sight, but I heard others say it was old Henry Carpenter, who had lost his wife and three children to the pox so many years before, and had never married again but only lived alone with his sorrow.

I remember asking where my poppet was, and Papa saying I ought not to think of such things now, for we had lost everything. But children are not sensible creatures. Will stormed about, threatening to go to Brutanna and kill everybody there, and I wept for my poppet, and for my kitten, and for Henry Carpenter, and for all that had once been comfortable and familiar and was now destroyed.

I know not how we rebuilt our houses and the mill and the bridge and all the rest, nor how we survived that winter with our harvest gone. I know we stayed on at the duke's castle for many months, and most likely it was he who fed us. Such things are the business of grown people, who look ahead and plan and build. I only felt the terrible loss, and the nightly fear that they would come back again—those bad men, those cruel strangers.

I could not understand what had made them travel so far to burn our little village, when they did not even know us and we had never done them any harm. It was a big question for such a small girl. I never did find the answer.

## 6

# PRINCE JULIAN
# OF MORANMOOR

*W*hen Bella was six, her interest turned to fairies. She claimed to have seen them in the twilight out upon the meadow. Will told her that they were only glowworms, but Bella said no, she had watched them from up close, and they were beautiful and had golden hair and wings like dragonflies and wore silver robes, and many other particulars. I know not where she got such ideas. Not from her family, of that I am quite sure. I think she just made things up as she went along—and yet she seemed truly to believe them.

One day I got the notion that Will and I ought to build a little fairy castle for her, down by the river, to see her amazement and delight when she beheld it. And so we set to work upon it, meaning only to make it a simple thing and be done with it in an afternoon. But first Will suggested we pave the courtyard with river pebbles, then I said we ought to have proper crenellations, and a portcullis for the entrance, and a moat with a drawbridge—and before long we had made something quite grand and not unlike my uncle's castle (though very much smaller).

The moat was a problem at first, for each time we filled it the water soaked away into the ground. Then Will thought to line the moat with reeds and pebbles, and this kept the water in.

Each day I would bring with me some bit of fancy stuff to decorate the castle—a strip of red silk for a banner, some patterned velvet for a tapestry, and the like. I took great pleasure in the most delicate work, such as making the little portcullis out of sticks and twine. Indeed, I found I was quite cunning with my hands, a gift I had not known I possessed until then.

When it was almost finished, Will remarked that he thought it looked like a very *good* castle, but that aside from being so small, it did not seem particularly fairylike.

"We cannot find any *real* fairies, Will," I told him.

"No, but we might catch some glowworms and put them inside."

I thought that over. I did not see how we could

keep them inside unless we closed the little shutters, and then Bella would not be able to see them, and most likely they would die in there.

"I do not think that would work, Will," I said. "We must think of something else."

That night, as I was drifting off to sleep, I had a great inspiration. I would tie a bit of string to the bottom of the little entry door, run it down under the ground through a conduit, and out to a place beyond the outer walls. I would make a loop at the far end so I could pull the string with my thumb—over to the side where Bella would not notice it—and the door would appear to open magically of its own accord!

"That is most ingenious," Will said the next day when I showed him my idea. "But what will she see inside when the door has opened? If we cannot make any fairies and you do not want to use glowworms?"

"I have thought of that, too," I said. And I told him.

At last we were ready to show Bella her great surprise. I said the king of the fairies and all his court were staying at his castle nearby, that I had spoken with him the day before, and that the king was most anxious to meet the beautiful Princess Bella—only we had to make haste, for they would not be staying long. The fairies had urgent business in the north and must be away soon.

"Oh! Oh!" she cried, dancing about with excitement, covering her mouth with her little hands. "Let us go now!" And she raced away, down toward the river.

We caught up with her and told her she must not run. She should walk slowly and show respect, for these were no ordinary fairies, but the king and all his court. She squeezed my hand and looked up at me and said, "I will, I will." Thereafter she walked so solemnly she might have been following a funeral procession to the churchyard.

"There it is, Bella!" I said as we neared the riverbank. (I kept firm hold of her hand, lest in her excitement she fall upon the castle and ruin it.) "Now approach carefully and kneel down, as is fitting." I felt her tremble—and such expressions of amazement and suppressed glee and even a little fear crossed her face! She kept her lips pressed together to keep from speaking or crying out, poor thing.

"You can whisper," I said.

"Oh, look, look, look!" she said (in a whisper that could be heard from the top of the rise), pointing out every feature of our creation. She admired the drawbridge and the guard towers, crying, "Oh! A portcullis, just like Castle Down!" (She had by then forgotten to whisper and was beginning to bounce and wiggle.) I looked at Will and saw that his face—

like mine—was flushed with pride. Strange as this will sound, that day remains in my memory as one of the grandest of my youth.

Bella began tugging on my sleeve. "Julian," she said, "I want to see the fairies now! Are they inside?"

"They must be," I said. "I suppose we ought to knock, though, don't you?"

She agreed that we ought, so I tapped gently upon the door with my finger. I waited a few seconds, then slowly pulled the little string, and the door magically opened. Bella shrieked with joy and leaned over to peer inside.

I had made tiny furniture for the great hall—a trestle table and little benches and a king's chair covered in red velvet. On the table lay a silver thimble and a note on parchment, written in strange characters. I delicately slid my fingers inside and drew it out.

"Can you read this, Will?" I asked.

"I cannot read at all, Julian," he answered. "Not even common writing, as you know—and this looks something strange."

We all studied it with great interest. Then I told Bella that I knew a *bit* of fairy writing, though not much. I would try to puzzle it out. So I looked at it awhile, Bella hanging on to my arm, her face eager and glowing with excitement.

"Here," I said, "I think I have made something of

this. It is from the king. He says he is most disappointed that we did not come in time, for they had to leave with the dawn this very day. But he wishes Bella to enjoy his hospitality, though he be not here to offer it in person. And so he has left behind a flagon of ale. The king regrets that it is so small, for he understands that humans are very big and drink great quantities — but, sadly, it is the largest they possess."

I handed Bella the thimble. She took it carefully between two fingers and solemnly drank the few drops it contained. Then she held it in her hand for a moment, gazing at it with a reverence worthy of the crown jewels. At last, as if responding to some inner command, she took a deep breath, squared her shoulders, and placed the thimble back upon the table.

"Wait!" I said. "Here is a postscript: 'Please tell Princess Bella that I would be most honored if she would keep the flagon as a token of my esteem.'"

How she smiled then, her eyes wide with wonder and amazement! Once again she reached her little fingers through the door, this time to retrieve her prize. She clutched it to her heart with both hands and looked up at me with an expression of perfect rapture. I thought it remarkable that such a small gift could produce so much joy. It pleased me enormously — and indeed, I do believe that at that moment I was every bit as happy as she was.

Our little castle was destroyed in the first hard rain thereafter, and Bella never did get to meet the king of the fairies, of course. But the thimble remained her greatest treasure. Beatrice sewed a little pouch for it, and Bella wore it round her neck always—even when she was a grown girl and had long ceased thinking of fairies.

I often wondered, in those later years, whether Bella had figured it out—that I was the one who had given her the thimble. I rather hoped so. I liked to think that she went on wearing it out of affection for me.

## 7

# MAUD

*I* waited three years before returning to Edward's house. I did not relish going there, you may be sure. But I longed to see Isabel again, and as I had been the one to carry her away after Catherine died, I thought I would offer to bring her home again.

Edward heaved a great, heavy sigh when I was ushered into his presence. I found him less distraught than when I had seen him last, but he still did not look well. It was as if he had—how shall I say this?—*dried up*, like a grape in the sun. No, no, that is not right, for a grape grows sweeter as it shrivels into a raisin, and such was not the case with Edward. Perhaps it would be better to say he had *spoiled*, like last week's table scraps.

He did not rise to greet me when I entered the room, nor did he offer me a seat, but I took one anyway.

"What brings you here?" he asked, with no attempt at courtesy.

"Your daughter," I answered. "Isabel. I was thinking that by now she is likely weaned, and as you may be occupied with other matters, you might wish me to go there and bring her home. I thought perhaps it would be more convenient for you."

"It is *not* convenient for me at all," he said. "I have no wife to attend to a child, as you well know, and no desire to have one in the house. I told you that before."

"But, Edward," I said, "she is living with *peasants*. They are goodly folk, truly, but it is no place for her to learn how to dress and how to behave in fine company and all that a wellborn child must know."

"Madam, it is none of your affair."

"But I am her aunt, Edward, and her godmother also!"

"Then you may pray for her soul, if you like."

"Indeed, I *do* pray for it already, Edward—every day—and do not need your permission to do so."

He sniffed and rose to his feet. I was being dismissed.

"Edward," I said, "I do not think it wise to leave her there much longer—she will pick up coarse habits that must only be broken later."

"Enough!" he said. "I told you already it was none of your affair. You know where the door is, Maud—it's the place where you came in."

"Only hear me a moment longer, Edward—"

"No, I will not! Isabel is *my* daughter, and I will dispose of her as I will!"

*"Dispose!"* I was aghast. How could he use such a word in connection with his own child?

"Oh, the devil take you," he roared, "you ugly, common, interfering busybody! Get out of my house and leave my daughter alone. Do you hear me? I will bring her home when I am ready, and not before. And if ever I have need of your assistance, *or* your opinions, you may be sure that I shall ask for them. Until that time, if I should hear that you are meddling in my affairs in *any* way, by God, I shall have you taken up by the law. And do not think I won't, out of sentiment for your sister—for I married her *despite* her family. And I have absolutely no wish to continue the acquaintance."

"You were happy to continue your acquaintance with our father's *money!*" I shouted back. I never should have said it—satisfying though it was—for my words were like bellows to a flame. He flashed out at me, so that I feared he might strike me. I took up my mantle in haste and moved quickly toward the front entrance.

"I will gladly raise her, if you will not," I said from the safety of the doorway.

"You will not so much as *speak* to her, do you hear me? I would rather she live with *lepers* than with you!"

Then he slammed the door.

And so I went home that day and wept my heart out. Edward seemed determined to leave that poor child exactly where she was. Whether he did it out of lunacy or spite, I never knew, but it mattered not. Either way Isabel would grow up a peasant, with no education and none of the skills or social graces expected of a highborn lady. How, then, was she to find her place in the world? Was she to marry a cobbler or a blacksmith? Or some down-at-the-heels knight who would wed her for her fortune and treat her with scorn? No one *else* would have her, of that I was quite sure—not with her coarse speech and common ways.

Hard as I tried, I could not drive the picture from my mind of my own dear sister's child out hoeing the garden, or shearing the sheep, or slopping the pigs, or plucking a chicken—work fit only for the lowest servant in my house. She would wear some awful, shabby gown, filthy, patched, and torn. Her skin would be ruined by the sun. Her hands would be calloused and filthy, with dirt beneath the nails. And her hair—so golden and downy soft when she was a babe—would be greasy and unkempt, hanging down in her face and blown about by the wind.

But then I checked myself, remembering her foster mother, good Beatrice, and how clean and well-ordered her cottage had been, and how tenderly she had held the child that day. And so I amended the vision somewhat. Now I saw Isabel running about on the common with the other children, barefoot and laughing. I saw her busy with useful tasks—spinning by the hearth, helping in the kitchen—and I began to grow rather fond of this imagined child. She was strong and eager and inclined to laughter. She held her head high, and her eyes were bright. She still wore a shabby gown, but at least it would be clean. And though she would not know her letters, she would have learned her prayers and her catechism. That was the best that even sensible Beatrice could manage. She could not give Isabel anything she did not herself possess.

And thus my thoughts returned once more to Edward and how he meant to deny his own daughter her birthright as a noble child. And I pictured Isabel once again, this time as she *ought* to have been. She was beautiful, of course, much like Catherine in her younger days. She sat beside the fire in the great hall of Edward's house with her sewing in her lap, wearing a fine silk gown and dainty slippers. Her hair was neatly plaited and coiled and covered with a linen veil. Her skin was smooth and white, her hands long and slender.

I moved closer, in my mind, so that I might study her face. But what I saw there made me gasp. For this child's eyes were not bright, but gazed dully down at her embroidery. Her shoulders were slumped and her expression wary. This girl, growing up in Edward's dark shadow, was a cowed and timid creature—fearful, lonely, and sad.

"You *simpleton*!" I shouted, and smote myself upon the leg. "You perfect and utter *fool*!" And I laughed, then, and clapped my hands. And then I got down upon my knees and thanked God with all my heart that I had failed in my mission to bring her home.

# PRINCE JULIAN
# OF MORANMOOR

For my tenth birthday, my father sent me a marvelous horse. I wonder if he even remembered how old I was, that he should send me such a beast. It was a huge black warhorse, eighteen hands high, and worth an absolute fortune!

My father had not seen me more than five or six times in all my life. Perhaps he had confused me in his mind with one of my older brothers, thinking I was tall and strong like John, a skilled rider and a champion upon the field. Of course I would have liked to be those things, but I was not. I was slight of build and small of stature, awkward and ungainly—and I was especially timid and inept when it came to horses. My usual mount was a small and patient mare, well past her youth and exceedingly docile. Thus, when my gift arrived and was led out onto the field, pawing and snorting, the master of the horse rolled his eyes in despair.

But I did not understand how inappropriate it was for me to own such a creature, or how impossible that I should try to ride him. I was too busy enjoying the envy of my fellow pages as they beheld my prize. I even went so far as to name him Bucephalus, after the famous horse of Alexander the Great. Oh, how it shames me to remember it now! I demanded to have him saddled immediately, so that I might ride him then and there.

The master of the horse answered my request by saying—in the hearing of all the other pages—that he thought I was not *near* ready to handle such an animal, if indeed I ever would be. I flushed scarlet at this reproach and was so overcome with righteous anger that I did a thing I had never done before: I pulled rank on my master.

"*My father*," I said with a piercing gaze, "*King Raymond*, desires that I should have this horse, and has sent him here so that I might ride him."

"*Your father*," the master responded with the icy calm of a man who has had his fill of arrogant little boys, "has entrusted me with the *chore* of teaching you to ride. And he *desires* that you should *survive* that education. And had he seen you jousting yesterday, my lord prince, he would have sent you a *mule* instead."

Oh, the silence that followed that remark! Had I been any other boy, they would all have howled with laughter. Instead, they gazed intently at their boots and endeavored to control their expressions. I spun upon my heels and strode away, boiling with rage and humiliation.

At dinner my uncle brought up the subject of the horse, for he knew nothing of my quarrel with the master, but only meant to make pleasant conversation. I knew not how to answer him except to say that it was a very fine animal indeed. The other boys bit their lips or turned away—all but Geoffrey of Brennimore, who smiled.

Was he *mocking* me?

I could not bear to think that he found me ridiculous, for Geoffrey was my ideal, the boy I longed to be. He was the best liked and most accomplished of all the pages, and upon the practice field he was unbeatable. He was a natural athlete, steady with a lance, quick and deadly with a sword—and how he could ride! I could not help but think that had *his* father sent *him* a warhorse, the master would have had the beast saddled right away.

Thus it was that Geoffrey's mysterious smile set

something stirring in me that went beyond caution and reason. After dinner that afternoon, I announced to the other pages that I would ride Bucephalus if it killed me!

Such insubordination, such defiance—especially considering my princely rank and my timid behavior on most occasions—caused a great stir among the pages. *This* was going to be an *event*!

Having assured ourselves that the master of the horse was occupied elsewhere, we made our way out to the stables. I thought Bucephalus seemed much calmer than he had in the morning, though he was every bit as large as before. I began to think I would have no difficulty in controlling him. Indeed, I was already imagining how I would tell the master afterward of my easy success, how I would make him eat his words.

We saddled Bucephalus in the stall; then I mounted him and rode out onto the practice field. How unlike my placid little mare he was! Every muscle in his mighty frame was trembling with restrained force! Oh, he would *go* all right, if I would but let him!

I rode Bucephalus in a circle, at an easy trot, and the boys cheered me on. I felt right wonderful, then, and proud, and confident, and so I urged the horse into a gallop. And, oh, the speed and the power and the sense of myself transformed into a champion, a hero—it filled me with a joy such as I had never known in all my life! I was Alexander of old, riding off to fight the Parthians! I was the Worthy Knight, galloping into the fray to bring great armies to their knees!

My head in the clouds, my soul on fire, I was lost to all reason—and so I gave Bucephalus another good prick with my spurs.

Had I been struck by lightning or swept down a mighty river in flood, I could not have been more astonished or unprepared. The horse shot forth like a bolt from a crossbow. That I kept my seat at all was a miracle, though I lost the reins and one of my stirrups and only held on by clutching his neck with all the strength in my arms. I think I was probably screaming, but the only sound I remember is the thunder of his hooves. I could not stop him, nor did I think I could stay upon his back much longer. I was too terrified even to consider how miserably I had disgraced myself.

Then, off to the side, I spotted a blur of color, and I began to hear the hooves of *another* horse pounding the earth. I dared not turn my head—it was plastered to the sweaty neck of my mount—but I could look back somewhat by moving my eyes. And what I saw was Geoffrey, come to my rescue! We rode side by side for a moment, for his horse was hard-pressed to pass Bucephalus, who thought it was a race. But after a bit, Geoffrey gained enough ground to grab hold of my reins. Gradually we slowed to a trot and finally halted. I realized only then that, out of the necessity for speed, Geoffrey had managed my rescue without even a saddle upon his horse!

I was not sure at that moment if I could ever forgive him for saving my life—and with such grace, and ease, and good humor! I had made myself look a fool; Geoffrey, by comparison, made me look far worse.

We returned to shouts of "well done!" and "hurrah!"—all of them much deserved, though not by me. I dismounted with trembling legs and managed not to weep, but only just. I left the others to unsaddle my great horse, rub him down, and put him away. I was so full of shame I could not bear to be in their company. And so I walked out the castle gates and into the village, tears running down my face. I wiped them away with dirty hands, making mud streaks upon my cheeks.

I went to the one place where comfort was to be had—the cottage of my old nurse. I found Bella there, in the yard, pounding away at the butter churn. All the cats in the neighborhood seemed to be there, hoping for an accident.

"Prince Julian!" Bella cried, abandoning her work and running to greet me.

"Princess Bella!" I answered, as I always did—though my voice was so strained with feeling, I knew not if she even heard me.

"Oh, Julian," she said, when she drew nearer and saw the evidence of tears upon my face. "What is the matter?"

"Oh, I have done something foolish, Bella," I said, "that is all."

"We *all* do foolish things; that's what Mama says."

"Aye, Bella, that is true—but some of us are more foolish than others." At this a fresh stream of hot tears coursed down my cheeks.

"Well, you must confess it then, and I will play the priest and give you absolution."

I laughed at that, for there never was anyone less solemn and priestlike than bright little Bella.

"Come and sit with me in the yard," she said, taking my hand. "And you must tell me everything, or else I will not sleep for a week from wondering."

"I think *I* shall not sleep for a week from remembering," I said. "But you shall hear it and must only promise not to laugh too heartily at my foolishness."

"Oh, I never would," she said most earnestly. "You know that!"

We sat, as so often we had before, upon the low wall at the side of the cottage. By habit we both began picking daisies and weaving them into flower crowns as we talked. The cats came over to see what we were about, then, finding nothing of interest, drifted back to investigate the churn, and finally went away.

"Father Bella," I said, "I have committed the sin of pride."

"Indeed?" she said with a grin.

"Indeed. My father sent me a gift today—a great beast of a warhorse. But the master said I was not yet skilled enough to ride him. And I was so mortified by what he said—and so full of pride—that I rode him anyway."

"But he is yours. Surely you can ride him whenever you want!"

"Yes, that is true."

"So?"

"I had to be rescued."

"Oh," she said, fighting a smile. "By the master? Was he terribly angry?"

"No, the master was not there. I was rescued by Geoffrey of Brennimore, a lad of my own age. He did it without even saddling his horse. Whereas I only just managed to stay on my great warhorse by clinging to his neck for dear life. I looked a perfect fool, Bella!"

"Oh, Julian," she said, touching my hand gently. "What if you had fallen? You might have been killed!"

"There was a moment this afternoon when that

seemed like a happier outcome."

"Now that *is* a foolish sentiment, indeed," she said. "And I suppose it *is* prideful as well. But I still do not think you are in need of absolution. You have been punished enough already."

"I'm afraid there's more. Bella, do you know what *hubris* means?"

She shook her head. "No. I do not know any Latin."

"It's Greek, actually. It means great pride, out of all reason. Foolish pride."

"But . . ."

"Bella, I named my horse Bucephalus."

She shrugged.

"Bucephalus was the horse of Alexander the Great. That was bad enough, but at least you might imagine I was only praising the horse. And he is a fine creature, deserving of a fine name. But, Bella, when I got upon his back and seemed to be riding him so well, I began to imagine *myself* as Alexander. Truly, Bella, I did!"

"And was he a great man? Alexander?"

"Oh, indeed, Bella, just as his name implies. He conquered the world!"

"Ah!"

"And then, Bella, I was not satisfied with merely playing a great hero. I imagined myself the *Worthy*

*Knight*! Is *that* not prideful enough for you? Can you picture *me* riding into the midst of a battle and bringing armies to their knees?"

"If God willed it, you could! You have a pure heart, Julian, as the Worthy Knight is said to have. God could make you a champion if it was needful. Who *knows* what He has planned for you?"

"Oh, Bella. Will you *always* see only the *best* in people?"

"I see you as you are." Then, making the sign of the cross over me, she said, "Prince Julian of Moranmoor, I hereby absolve you of the great sin of having *too much imagination*!"

I laughed. "*And* being prideful," I added.

"That, too," she said. "If you insist."

# BELLA

*I*n those dismal years after we said good-
bye (or rather did *not* say good-bye, but
parted all the same), I thought often of that
afternoon down by the river. It was how I
always wished to remember him—not as he
was that last time, when he broke my heart.

I was watching Margaret for Mother, who
was busy with the threshing. We had gone to
the riverbank with our baskets, in search of
herbs for the making of simples for such mal-
adies as rashes of the skin or aching joints or
pain in the head. I have a good eye for
plants—Mother has often said so. It was she
who taught me which herbs to look for and
how to recognize them, what were the seasons

for each, and whether to pick them at midday or at night by moonlight, so they would have more potency.

The weather was fair and warm, so Margaret and I took off our shoes and sat in the grass by the side of the river, our feet dangling in the cool water. A flock of ducks were feeding on plants in the shallows, upending themselves in the process, heads down in the water, rear ends pointing at the sky. Margaret found this most comical; she was easy to entertain.

Then, over the sounds of wind and river and the soft conversation of ducks, there came a cry of "hoo-hoo!" I looked up and here came Julian, riding over the hill on the far side of the river. He reined in his horse at the crest of the rise and remained there, unmoving, his back erect, his head high, and a falcon upon his fist. I secretly wondered if perchance he was posing thus so that we might admire him and notice how he sat his mount so well (it was that big, black horse of his, the one with the important name). Certainly I was glad enough to admire him, if he wished. He did look noble indeed. I waved and called his name.

Just then a brace of hounds came thrashing through the high grass in our direction, straight at the ducks. At the same moment, the falcon spread her great wings and rose into the air, where she circled above Julian's head, awaiting his command.

Before I could draw a breath, the ducks had seen the dogs and erupted out of the water, filling the air with their cries of alarm and the thunderous beating of wings. Then the falcon struck, diving straight as an arrow at one of the ducks, grasping it tight in her murderous claws.

Margaret climbed onto my lap and hid her face, peering around now and again to see what more would happen. Across the river I saw Julian dismount and retrieve the prize from his falcon. Then he gave a command, and she perched back upon his fist again. I marveled at how tame she seemed, as obedient as one of his hounds.

"Prince Julian!" I called again.

"Princess Bella!" he answered. "Lady Margaret!"

Julian climbed back into the saddle and rode across the river, so as not to spoil his boots. Then he came and sat down upon the bank, a bit apart from us. "Be as still as you can," he said in a soft voice, stroking the falcon's feathers. "Let her become accustomed to you." She watched us uneasily with her large, dark eyes.

Slowly Julian reached into the hunting bag with his other hand and came out with a small leather hood, crowned by a delicate plume of feathers. I watched, amazed, as he slipped it gently over the falcon's head, covering her eyes. She ruffled her feathers, then, and grew still.

"There!" Julian said, grinning. "All is well. She thought you were quite terrifying, but now that you've gone, she feels safe."

"But we *haven't* gone," said Margaret.

"Ah, but she *thinks* you have. She knows the world only through her eyes. If she cannot see you, then you are not there. You can stroke her now, if you want. But be gentle."

I guided Margaret's hand, and together we caressed her wing. She seemed not to mind and appeared completely docile. But I had seen her fly and hunt and knew her to be a wild and dangerous creature. And so it thrilled me to touch her and feel the softness of her beautiful feathers.

"Is she new?" I asked. "What's her name?"

"You always ask two questions at once, Bella! But as to the first—yes, she is new. A birthday gift from my father."

"I had not known it was your birthday!"

"Well, it was. I turned sixteen. Now I am terribly old."

"Did you go up to the palace for your birthday?"

"That's *three* questions now, and I have only answered the first!"

I bit my lip and crossed my arms. I would not speak, *ever again*.

"To answer your *second* question," he said, "before I go on to the *third*—I have named her Princess."

"After me?" (Alas, I forgot!)

"That's four. Will you have me answer them in any particular order?"

"As you please," I said. I would not say *another word*.

"All right. Yes, I have been to the palace. And yes—though I know quite a lot of princesses, the one I was thinking of when I named my falcon was Princess Bella."

I sat for some time not speaking, just to show him I could do it. Then I said, "Thank you."

"You are most welcome. You have a lot in common. It seemed fitting."

I started counting upon my fingers: "I am not a bird. I am not a fierce, wild creature. I do not have yellow feet or a sharp, cruel beak. I cannot fly, and I will *not* perch upon your fist!"

Julian exploded with laughter. I had not meant to be funny. "You are not a bird," he agreed, between guffaws. "I cannot speak to the yellow feet and the other things."

"Well," I said, rather stiffly—once he had stopped gasping and sniffling and wiping his eyes as though the laugh had all but sent him to his grave—"your falcon is indeed beautiful. And since you have been *very* rude, and since you have raised the subject of princesses and claim to know so many, you must now entertain us by telling us all about them."

"Sweet Bella, they are *nothing* compared to you."

I blushed. "I am not truly a princess," I said, "as you perfectly well know. I want to hear about the *real* ones."

"I can't understand why—they are awfully dull. But if I must—let me see. There is Princess Berta, who is married to my eldest brother, John. As he is heir to the throne, Berta will someday be queen, and so she behaves in a very queenly manner."

"Elegant and high-minded?"

"No, pompous, conceited, and arrogant. And before you ask if she is beautiful,"—I confess, I was about to—"she is bony and whey-faced with a large nose and a weak chin."

"Ugh," I said. "How disappointing. Does she have no admirable qualities?"

"Her pedigree is impeccable. A princess twice over, by birth and by marriage."

"Have you nothing better to offer?"

Julian sighed. "There is Princess Alana, wife of my brother Gilbert. He was intended for the church, being the second son. But it soon became clear that he was not suited for the priesthood. He is not devout, for one thing, nor is he much of a scholar. In truth, my brother Gilbert is rather weak-minded. And so naturally my father chose him a wife who is very pious and reads philosophy all day. How they bear each other, I cannot imagine. And no, not beautiful either. Are you bored?"

"Is there not a third princess? You have another brother."

"Laurent has no princess. He went into the church in Gilbert's place. And *I*, as you know, have *two* princesses, and they are the best of the lot."

"Julian?" I said, a new thought having suddenly come to me. "Will you not soon have a real princess of your own—now that you are sixteen and so very old? Will your father not find you a wife?"

"I suppose one day he is bound to find me some tedious, prune-faced duchess with a huge dowry and the right political connections. But as he has not thought overmuch about me heretofore, perhaps he will *go on* not thinking about me for a while longer. Like as not, I will go off to war and die in Brutanna before ever he gets around to it."

"Oh, horrible!" I cried. "Do not say such things!"

"Well, it was *you* who brought up the prune-faced duchess," Julian said, grinning and rising to his feet. The dogs, which had lain contentedly nearby, drying themselves from their swim in the river, now leaped up and wagged their tails excitedly.

"I never said 'prune-faced,'" I corrected him. "Don't go!"

"Princess Bella—Lady Margaret—I must. I promised my other Princess a day of hunting to sharpen her skills, and all I have allowed her is a single duck." Julian mounted his horse and carefully removed the hood from Princess's eyes. Then he smiled down at us, all set to ride away.

"Prince Julian," I said. "You will come back soon?"

"Princess Bella, I could not stay away."

# PRINCE JULIAN
# OF MORANMOOR

*I* woke that morning while it was yet dark, too excited to sleep. My uncle had given us leave to go to the Middleton Fair, and though the master of the horse would accompany us (to keep us out of trouble, and to buy some new horses for the duke's stable), I did not think even *his* long face and gruff manner could spoil our fun. Not with all that tasty food and special ale—and the jugglers, and acrobats, and fire-eaters, and Gypsy fiddlers, and so many trinkets to buy!

We set out before dawn, the master riding in the lead, stiff and unsmiling as ever, and in his wake a pack of boisterous boys on the cusp of manhood, eager for a bit of excitement. We had left early in hopes of making some headway before the roads became congested, but we were too late. Already they were filled with wagons and handcarts and wheelbarrows and horses and sheep—indeed, it seemed as though every village in the region had emptied itself out onto that road, and that all the world was going to Middleton Fair!

We wove our way through the traffic as best we could, waving gaily and calling out greetings to those we passed. By the time we reached the boundary stone of Middleton, the sun was well up in the sky and our tunics were coated with dust from the road.

We stabled our horses at the edge of town and continued on foot, though our progress was slow because of the crush of people. The master of the horse urged us to stay together and to be wary of pickpockets; they were sure to be about in such a crowd, with all of us pressed together as we were, and everyone carrying money to spend at the fair.

The narrow streets were lined with stalls selling all manner of goods—honey and hides, copper pots and salt fish and finely woven cloth. Tailors and carpenters and cobblers were there, ready to make you some new clothes or mend your furniture or resole your boots. There were sticky sweets to buy and some exceptional ale, made especially for the fair. But the master of the horse was eager to get to the paddock before the best horses had been sold, so he would not allow us to linger, gaping at the stalls and entertainments. "You shall have time enough for that later," he said.

We had a new boy with us that day, Rolf, a haughty and pompous lad who had taken it upon himself to keep order among the other boys. The smallest infraction of the rules, the most innocent prank, the slightest oath would earn us a reprimand from Rolf. And how eager he was to go running to the master with tales of our transgressions! Not surprisingly, nobody liked him much.

Now, as we made our way through the crowd, Geoffrey lost his balance and collided with this boy, throwing him in the path of a pretty country girl. She would have fallen had Rolf not reached out and caught her in his arms. He was mortified by this encounter and blushed scarlet, apologizing profusely. The girl blushed also and, wresting herself from his awkward embrace, accepted his apology and went upon her way.

I noticed Geoffrey grinning and winking at his friends. Not a minute later, the poor lad was once again shoved into the way of a passing lady. Again he reached out and caught her as before. But there was no pretending it had been an accident this time, so uproarious was the laughter of the other boys. The girl pulled away from his grasp and cuffed him hard upon the cheek.

Rolf turned toward Geoffrey in a rage. "Shame on you!" he said, to which we responded by laughing all the harder, slapping our thighs and holding our stomachs. The master of the horse was not amused by this sport. He grabbed Geoffrey by the arm and led him through the crowd like a felon on his way to prison.

We arrived at the paddock at last, and the master looked over the horses, finding several that he deemed worth buying. And so, while he was discussing terms with the seller, we sat upon the fence and watched the crowd.

Most of us were of an age, fifteen or sixteen, and had been promoted from page to squire. Our training had become more strenuous and challenging, and we would soon begin serving my uncle in battle. The prospect of danger and adventure to come had stirred up strange new feelings in us, and we were strung as tight as lute strings. Perhaps that is why we were so rowdy that day and inclined toward manly bravado. It did not take much to send us into wild bouts of laughter.

In this spirit Geoffrey began calling out to any pretty girl who passed our way, "Come here, my beauty! Give me a kiss!" and suchlike bold remarks. A few of them shook their heads in disgust and walked away, but many responded with shy smiles, for Geoffrey was a remarkably handsome lad, tall and broad shouldered with a goodly face and fine, golden hair. Girls always noticed him.

Indeed, there was only one who seemed truly offended by his gallantry. She announced, with her hands upon her hips, that she'd sooner kiss a hog! The crowd burst into applause at her wit, and we nearly fell off the fence with laughing. It was coarse and unchivalrous child's play—we all knew it—but it was enormous fun! And I was very much a part of it, swept up in the general hilarity and spirit of camaraderie.

It was just at that moment—as I was wiping tears of laughter from my face and searching the crowd for the next likely target of Geoffrey's affection—that I saw a familiar figure coming our way. And, oh, I felt sick at heart—for it was Bella! And truly, I did not want to see her. Not there, not in that place, with all those people around.

I had lived all my life in two separate worlds, and that had made me changeable. I had learned to alter myself to be like those around me, in hopes of being accepted and admired. And at that particular moment I was the *other* Julian, not the one who played with peasants. I truly could not talk to her with those boys watching.

As Bella came toward me in her faded gown and old straw bonnet—I blush to confess it now—I saw her through my comrades' eyes and was embarrassed. And so I turned my head away from her and raised my hand as if to shield my eyes from the sun, hoping thus to hide my face so she would not see me. But it did no good—I was sitting upon a fence, in a scarlet tunic, with a crowd of noisy boys. I could not have been more conspicuous.

"Prince Julian!" Bella cried, grinning and waving excitedly.

Geoffrey and the others looked at me, all amazement. What's this? Julian has a lady friend, and a pretty one, too? They began elbowing me merrily in the ribs and making rude noises, kissing and whistling and such.

This delighted me, for they had never treated me so intimately before. Indeed, I had long suspected they tolerated me only because of my princely birth. Yet now, by receiving Bella's attentions, I had passed some mysterious test of manhood. I was no longer a timid and clumsy boy, but had become a "right manly fellow," a "scoundrel," and a "rogue"—in short, the kind of boy they liked. Their acceptance felt good to me, and I was reluctant to lose it.

What's more, I knew exactly what would follow if I got down from that fence and went over to Bella and greeted her warmly as she expected me to (or, God forbid, if I called out "Princess Bella!" as I usually did). My companions would shower us with whistles and catcalls, thinking her the object of some base flirtation. And so I convinced myself that by staying where I was and pretending not to know her, I was merely protecting her from their rude attentions and low regard.

I nodded politely, as one does to a servant, then turned toward Geoffrey and shrugged. I am afraid I even said she was only some village girl I had seen once or twice. And he replied that perhaps I ought to hurry on down to the village and see her again, as she seemed so eager and was so comely.

When I turned back, Bella had gone.

She was out there in the crowd, I knew, her face flushed with anger, her cheeks wet with tears. She would think herself a world-class fool for having thought well of me, for believing I was steadfast and honorable in my character, and a loving friend. And she would tell Beatrice what I had done—and Martin, and Will, and even little Margaret—and they would despise me, too!

Suddenly I was overcome by the enormity of all I had lost—and I simply could not sit there any longer. I felt a desperate need to take action, to run and find Bella that very minute and beg her to forgive me—

though of course I would never find her in that crowd. The only sensible thing was to stay and enjoy the fair, then go see Bella after we returned. But that was impossible for me. I absolutely *had* to do something, anything, right away! And so I made up my mind to leave immediately and ride back to the village. I would be at her doorstep when she returned.

I told the others that I was feeling ill—and indeed I was, for shame sat in my stomach like a stone, and when the talk turned to food and ale I grew ashen and said I did not think I could eat or drink anything at all. And so I left the others and returned to where we had stabled our horses.

It did not take nearly so long to ride back as it had taken us to get there. The roads were clear by then, but for a few stragglers still on their way to the fair. And in my eagerness, I spurred Bucephalus on. I would not be cautious that day! I was wild in my spirit and cared not what became of me.

All the way I thought of little but what I would say to Bella. I rehearsed my story so many times that after a while it came to seem quite credible and persuasive to me, and I began to feel sure that, by the time the sun had set on that warm September day, Bella and I would be friends again and all would be forgotten.

But then, with a start, it came to me *why* my apology was so compelling, so sure to win her forgiveness:

*because it was not entirely true*! I had not planned to tell her *all* of the reasons why I had treated her so unkindly, but only the one that would make me look well in her eyes—that I had wished to spare her the attentions of my boisterous companions. Even as I sought to persuade her that I was a true friend and an honorable person, I would be telling her a lie!

I was so shaken by this realization that I forced myself to look deep inside my own character and face whatever I might find there. Never in my life had I been that honest with myself, and it was no easy thing for me to do. The wide chasm that gaped between the person I had thought myself to be and the person I truly was appalled me. I resolved, at that moment, that when I spoke to Bella I would tell her *all*—and if she would not forgive me, well, that was what I deserved.

Furthermore, I swore that from that day forward I would always strive to be as decent and honest as she had once thought me to be. Unchangeable Bella, with her unerring sense of who she was, her fixed inclination toward all that was good—she would be my north star. And truly, I *have* become better and continue striving still.

How cruel, then, was what happened next—the ill-timed summons that intervened and prevented me from going to Bella as I had planned, and abasing myself, and begging her forgiveness! In truth, I would take it for God's punishment—and well deserved, too—except that Bella suffered from it more than I did.

As I neared the village, you see, I was met upon the road by a messenger who had been riding out to fetch me home from the fair—and the news he carried was astounding. The great, endless war between Moranmoor and Brutanna, begun back in my great-grandfather's time, had ended, and a truce had been signed. And I, the all-but-forgotten son, had a crucial role to play in this momentous event: I was to be part of a royal hostage exchange, meant to ensure that the treaty was kept in good faith.

I would go to live at the royal court in Brutanna, while Prince Gerald, younger brother of King Harry Big Ears, would come to Moranmoor. Should either party take advantage of the truce to attack the other, the life of its royal hostage would be forfeit. And in fulfillment of this important role, I was commanded to leave at once for the King's City.

"I will go, and gladly," I said, for here was a chance to redeem myself and restore my honor. "But I must take a day—or even a few hours if that be not possible—to tend to a personal matter of great import."

"You cannot," the messenger said. "King Raymond wished you to leave without delay—already your absence at the fair has set our departure back by many hours."

"But I must see to my belongings, and that will take time. Can we not leave at daybreak tomorrow?"

"No, Your Highness, I fear not. Your things will be packed for you, to follow later. You may take a change of linen if you like, and whatever you can gather quickly and carry on your person. But we must make haste."

I had no choice. I must bid a hurried farewell to my uncle and be away within the hour. By the time Bella returned from the fair, I would already be gone. I thought, at first, that I should *write* my apology and leave the letter at the cottage, awaiting their return. But Bella could not read. Nor could any in the family. They would take it to the priest to have it read aloud, and this I could not bear.

And so I rode away from Castle Down and the village, and the life I had known for sixteen quiet years. I carried with me only my sword, some clean linen, and a great weight of sorrow and regret. I was not given the chance to ask the forgiveness of my dearest friend, whom I had injured out of pride and selfishness—or even to tell her good-bye. After all those years of loving friendship, my parting gift to her was the bitter memory of my unkindness.

# BELLA

*Y*ou will think me a fool not to have
expected it, Julian being so far above me,
and no longer a child. But I did not. I never
thought it mattered to him that I was a peasant,
unlettered and common—for did he not come
to see us often, and speak warm words, and in
so many other ways show me his particular
regard? Ignorant as I was, I thought it all genuine. I never doubted we would always be
friends. But I suppose it was only one of my
childish fancies, like believing in fairies.

How could I have been so blind? Only a
simpleton would think a royal prince could
truly esteem a peasant. People such as us were
put on earth to haul water and cook food and

empty the chamber pots of such as him! I ought to have been grateful he even remembered my name! That I should have expected him to *introduce me to his friends* —was I out of my mind?

Oh, how far I had overstepped my bounds—I blushed to think of it! Indeed, I had made such a fool of myself over Julian that he had actually *laughed* about it to his friends—and right there in front of me, too, where I could not help but hear him! Either he *intended* to wound me, or he did not think it mattered— I am not sure which of the two is more horrible.

I was so filled with shame and mortification after that day at Middleton Fair that I could not bring myself to speak of it, not even to my parents, not even to Will. When we heard that King Raymond had called Julian home and that he was being sent to Brutanna, I let them believe that was the reason for my tears. To this day I never *have* told them otherwise.

Losing Julian shifted the foundation upon which I had built my life. It was like the time, so many years before, when the soldiers first came to our village: one moment I was secure in my understanding of the world, and then suddenly all my certainties collapsed. If I had been so badly mistaken about Julian, what other fondly held beliefs would prove to be false?

Oh, heaven help me—I was soon to find out!

I was returning home from the mill one afternoon,

Mother having sent me there with a sack of grain to be ground into flour. It was October, and the air was sharp and cool, the sky a rich, deep blue, and the smell of smoke and apples was in the air. As I neared the cottage, I paused for a moment and looked back down the lane where the slanting sunlight glowed through the yellow leaves—and I was suddenly so overcome by the beauty of God's creation that I almost wept. It was the first time since Julian left that I had felt true joy, and I shall always remember it— that final gift, that brief moment of peace.

Then I opened the cottage door to find my whole family there, most unexpectedly, at a time when Father and Will should have been at the forge and Mother busy with her tasks. I saw someone else in the room, too—a rather plump, grand-looking lady I had not met before. They were all waiting for me, that was plain enough. The first thing I thought was, somebody has died!

"Come in, Bella," Mother said. "Do not look so alarmed. I would like you to meet someone. This is your Auntie Maud, child. Will you curtsy to her nicely, as I taught you?"

I curtsied—but I was wary, for I knew something strange was afoot. All in the room were ill at ease. They had something to tell me, and they did not like to do it.

"Bella, do you understand what that means," Mother prompted, "that she is your aunt? This good lady is the *sister* of your *mother*."

I stood there, pondering this information. "Your sister?" I asked, knowing as I said it that she could not be.

"No, dear." Mother glanced at Father, then at the lady, then went on. "You see, in truth I am only your *foster* mother. Your *real* mother died when you were born."

"My real mother . . . ," I repeated stupidly.

"Her name was Catherine," said the lady who was now to be called "Auntie."

They watched as I began to grasp the implications of what I had just learned. I looked at Father, searchingly.

He only nodded sadly.

And so that meant that Will and Margaret were not my brother and sister! I took a sudden breath, for somehow that was the hardest news of all. They were *mine*! They were part of me!

"Oh, Bella!" Mother-who-was-not-Mother said, kneeling down and taking my hands in hers.

"And my real father?" I asked. "Is he dead also?"

"No, child."

Now the lady spoke again. "You see, your mother was a perfect angel, and your father loved her so much that when she died, he was much disordered by grief. And so I brought you here, to this good place, until such time as your father was fit to look after you."

"Why did no one *tell* me?" I cried. I was weeping now, and cared not that all were watching me. "How could you let me believe you were my family when you were not? Did *you* know, Will? Did even *Margaret* know?" I did not allow them to answer, for I fell upon the floor and screamed and wailed—I was so broken-hearted and I was so angry!

The auntie rose as if to come and comfort me, but I shouted at her not to touch me, not to come near, and so she sat down again. They let me cry until I was spent. Then I sat up and looked around at all of them and said, "You ought to have told me!"

"Yes," Father said. "We ought to have done. Truly, Bella, we *meant* to."

Now, looking at the auntie, I went on being shrewish with all the force I had in me. "And *you* have come here—why? Because this *father* of mine, this *father* . . . has he a name?"

"Edward."

"This *father*, this *Edward*, who sent me away as a tender child and has never *once* come to see me or inquired after me . . ." Here I began to weep again.

"That is why we could not bring ourselves to tell you, child," Mother said.

"This *father*," I wailed (I *would* finish my thought!), "has he now decided that I must leave this house where I am happy and these people I love and believed to be my family and go live with him?"

"Yes, child."

"Where? Where am I to go?"

"To the King's City," said the auntie. "He has a fine big house there, Isabel. He is a knight."

"*A knight!* I am a *knight's* daughter? Oh, wonder of wonders! How unfortunate Prince Julian did not know of this! A *knight's* daughter! What else?"

"Oh, there is much else," said the auntie—and I noticed that I liked the sound of her voice. "Of your sweet dear mother who held you in her arms and loved you so long ago, and did not deserve to die. Of that I can tell you much. We will talk of it on the road."

"And my father? Is there more to tell of *him*?"

"Some. Not so good to hear, I'm afraid. But he has married again, and I think his new wife will have softened him. And I will be nearby and will do all I can to ease your way."

"But why?" I asked. "Why does he send for me now, after so many years?"

All eyes turned to Auntie.

"Well," she said, "I confess he did not tell me his reasons. He sent a letter, is all, to ask would I go and fetch you home. But I would guess he has finally recovered his senses. And as he has a wife now, to keep house for him, it will be easier for him to do all for you that is proper and needful—and long overdue, Isabel."

"But I do not *want* to go," I wailed.

"Enough, Bella," Mother said then. "Stop your weeping. The bird leaves the nest, and so must you. We do not like it, either, for we have loved you as our own for all these years. But you are thirteen, now— almost a woman. You would have left us anyway before long, to marry and make a new life with your husband. It is well that you prepare yourself now to live according to your station, and know your own father and your good auntie here, while still you can."

This was so well said and sensible that I bowed my head in submission and agreed to do as I was bid. I set to gathering such few things as I had and made ready to leave the next morning.

Then, in what little time remained before dark, I went about the village and said good-bye to my friends of a lifetime. I told them that I had recently discovered I was a knight's daughter and that I was off to live in a grand house in the King's City—and I found I was rather taken with the idea. I wondered if they thought I was only making up stories, as I was wont to do as a child, but they seemed to believe me.

Well, of course, I thought! Of *course* they would know I was not born in that village, at least those who were old enough to remember when my auntie brought me there. Surely they had known it all along, yet they'd never said a word, except that they called me Princess. I saw now that it had been more than just a baby name. They called me that because of my noble birth. I never really was one of them.

That night, as I lay upon my pallet by the fire for the last time, I thought of my foster parents and how good they had been to me, how they had given me a home when my father would not, and how they had loved me as dearly as they loved their own children. It did not seem fitting, after that, to add my grief to theirs. And so the next morning, when it came time to leave, I kept my composure. I gave them my warmest love and thanks, then kissed them good-bye and rode away. Margaret ran along beside us for a time, throwing kisses. And people came out of their houses to wave good-bye. Auntie had given me a fur-lined mantle to wear against the cold—and I *did* feel like a knight's daughter in it. I liked that my friends saw me wearing it. I wondered if I would ever see them again.

We had been out upon the road for but a little time when Auntie reined in her horse and turned to me with a troubled look upon her face. "Dear child, I did not think!" she said. "Did you wish to go up to the castle and say your farewells to the prince?"

"How did you know about the prince?" I asked, my cheeks burning.

"Why, you spoke of him yesterday. And Beatrice told me what loving friends you were, from the time you were a wee babe! She mentioned it several times. I think she wished me to know that not *all* in your upbringing was so very humble. Shall we turn back, so that you may say good-bye to him?"

"No," I said, "for he is not there. He lives in Brutanna now, at the royal court. Did you never hear of it, Auntie? He is a hostage there, as part of the truce that ended the war."

"No, I never did!" she said. "You must think me a perfect dunce! But I do not get about much in the world. I look after your grandfather and have little time for gossip. I do know of the truce, of course. All the world knows about that. But, my stars—that poor fellow! Sent off to live in Brutanna!"

"What is so very dreadful about Brutanna, Auntie? He is living with the royal family there, in the palace—even though he *is* a hostage."

"Well, I suppose that in the palace they live better than the common folk. Perhaps they light the fire once or twice in the winter and do not spit upon the floor and eat fish guts and pigs' ears for dinner."

"Oh, Auntie—you are making up stories!"

She reached over, then, and took my hand in hers. It was warm, and dry, and soft, and it made my fingers tingle—and, strange as it is to tell, with that touch I felt the sorrow and the anger begin to drain away from me, and I felt whole again. I gasped at the wonder of it. She squeezed my hand and looked straight into my eyes. I saw that she was weeping.

"What happened?" I said.

"Oh, child, just one person loving another."

"No. Something more."

"Well," she said, "I do not know how to say this, but all my life people have told me that my touch brings them comfort. Your dear mother said it was so, and poor Father says it, also. I have always thought it foolishness—only, now I think perhaps I must believe it."

"Why, Auntie? Why now?"

"Because, dear Isabel, I felt it, too. From you."

"From *me*?"

"Such gift as I have—sweet Catherine said it was because I had lived a life of service and God had blessed me for it—my gift is a small thing compared to yours. I saw it in your eyes when you were born, and I felt it again just now."

"What do you mean?" I asked, stunned.

"I do not know, dear child. I do not know. We must wait and see."

# BOOK II

## *The Ring*

# ALICE

My father lies below the sea. Crabs scuttle over him and scatter his bones. Beside his remains, half buried in the sand, lie trinkets he was bringing home for me.

I rehearse this scene in my dreams, night after night. Mother says I'm being morbid. She says each day brings enough gloom and trouble without our hoarding it up and mooning over it. But can I help the dreadful thoughts that drift into my mind as I sleep?

Before Father left this last time, he invited us all to go down to the harbor and see the ship that would be his floating home for so many months. He would show us his snug little cabin, he said, with its slanted walls and tiny windows. And we could watch the sailors scrambling up the masts as nimbly as squirrels in the trees! Surely anyone would be eager for such an adventure. I certainly was.

But Mother said she has a weak stomach and could not tolerate the rocking of the ship (it was at anchor in a peaceful harbor). In truth, I think she feared she might get her gown wet about the hem or soil her shoes. As for Marianne, I suspect she was too occupied with her own affairs. She had an appointment with the dressmaker. Also she is inclined to worry about what damp air will do to her curls. But I did not care—it meant I would have Father all to myself.

We rode down to the harbor early in the morning. Along the way he told me stories of the faraway places he has seen, of the Moors who dress in long robes and wear turbans upon their heads and have another, completely different religion from ours. They do not drink ale or wine and are very particular about being clean—they bathe *every day* and yet do not fall ill or suffer any consequences from it at all!

He told me about some creatures of the desert, rather like horses with long legs and humps upon their backs. He said they could travel for days and days without drinking any water. He swore he had ridden them many times. They are trained to get down on their knees, he said, so you can climb up onto their backs. But they have nasty tempers and will spit at you if you do not take care.

In Egypt there are giant dragons in the rivers that can swallow you in a single gulp. Children from nearby villages go missing all the time. They just wade into the river and are swallowed whole! I shrieked when he told me that, so he took me in his arms and kissed my nose and said it was altogether too tiny and he needed to keep kissing it so it would grow properly. Soon I was laughing, and he was telling me about pirates. Then we arrived.

The harbor was full of so many ships—and such a profusion of tall masts rose up from them—that it made me think of a forest in wintertime.

"Oh, Father," I cried, "which one is yours?"

"Wait and see," he said. Then he took my hand and helped me into a little boat with some great, smelly sailors. Once we were settled, they rowed us away from the dock, past ship after ship, each one looming far above us, high as a castle wall.

Father's ship wasn't the biggest and it wasn't the grandest, but it was *Father's* ship and so I liked it the best. I craned my neck to see to the top. Men were leaning over the railing and looking down at us.

"How will we get up there?" I asked.

"You shall fly, little bird," Father said. Then he

called up to the men, "A bosun's chair for Cap'n Alice!" The faces went away and soon a chair appeared, lowered from on high by ropes. I got into it and held on tight, and they hauled me up on deck. Never in my life had I been so frightened—or so thrilled—all at the same time!

Father climbed a rope ladder. He did not need a chair.

Oh, you cannot imagine anything so grand as the deck of that ship! You could fit our great hall onto it four times over, perhaps more. And the wood on the deck was smooth and clean, not like at home where we have rushes on the floor, hiding the occasional dog's dropping or chicken bone. The sailors scrub the deck *every morning,* too—imagine that!

They were busy loading the ship with goods: a fortune in woolen cloth and glassware and port wine and other things that Father would trade for spices and silk and ebony and ivory. They also had to bring along food for the crew to eat during the voyage: barrels of herring and ale and hard bread and salt meat—and even ordinary water, for seawater is not wholesome to drink.

And the sailors truly *did* climb up the tall masts, just as Father had said they would. And they did not seem afraid to do it, either. I suppose they have to go up there all the time, for that's how they let out the great sails and take them in again.

"You ought to see them do it in a gale," Father said, grinning.

Suddenly a chill ran through me—a gale! I did not wish to imagine them being tossed about by a howling wind and crashing waves—but once he had spoken of it, I could not drive the image out of my thoughts. And from that moment on, the ship lost all its charms and came to seem horrid and dangerous to me. Father's little cabin became a death hole; I saw him trapped there, terrified, as water filled the room. I imagined the stout masts crashing down and splintering the deck below. Then I saw the hull crack open and men fall to their deaths into the boiling sea.

And I picture it still, every night, in my dreams. I wish I had never seen that ship.

# MARIANNE

As soon as Father returned, I was to be wed.

A girl cannot always count on liking the man she is to marry, but I did. Richard was tall and fair and near to my own age. He could just as easily have been sixty or twelve, foul breathed or snot nosed. I know that. But Father was content in his own marriage and desired that I might feel the same about mine. Besides, we were in a good bargaining position. Though Father was of the merchant estate, he was as rich as a lord, and Mother was the daughter of a knight. Even more to the point, Mother had not borne a living child in twelve years. Her chances of producing a son and heir were fast fading. It was likely that Alice and I would inherit everything.

Richard's eyes were a bit too close together, that is true, and his face a little prone to red spots — the sort of blemishes boys so often suffer from in their youth. But he would outgrow them in time, and aside from those minor flaws, he was as goodly a man as any girl could want. He still had a full head of hair and most of his teeth.

At the time of our marriage, Richard would dower me with a manor house and a village of more than five hundred souls — also the cattle and sheep and pigs, as well as the income from the mill, the bridge crossing, and the communal oven. This was more than acceptable, and I hoped through good management and wise investment to increase my holdings over time.

For my part, I would bring a dowry that was as exotic as it was splendid, and of this I was exceedingly proud. Though I had hemmed and embroidered the sheets myself, the bed hangings were of silk and gold brocade. I doubted even the *king* had anything so fine! And the saltcellar was of gold, studded with emeralds. My dresses were so beautifully made and of such rare fabrics that I believe I could have worn them at the king's court, and the greatest ladies in the land would have looked upon me with envy.

Our father traveled the world, and each time he

returned he brought us wonderful gifts—oh, what an eye for quality he had! Such jewels and ornaments of gold and embroidered silks and silver candlesticks of cunning design and rosewood boxes inlaid with ebony and ivory! And aromatic spices, too, and receipts for how to use them in exotic dishes. He entertained us with stories about the pashas and sultans of foreign lands. And so, by way of Father's travels, we grew far more worldly than our neighbors.

It was only natural, then, that my wedding feast should be a truly splendid affair, so lavish and elegant that for years thereafter people would still speak of it in hushed voices! Oh, the fancy dishes we would have the cooks prepare—rich delicacies never tasted before in our town! And our guests would not eat from trenchers like common folk, but from dishes of pure silver—one for each person, so they would not have to share. And all the guests would drink their wine from goblets of fine Venetian crystal!

Already our hall was decorated with beautiful tapestries and hangings, but Father promised to bring us yet more, in time for the wedding. We would drape swags and garlands of aromatic leaves and flowers upon the walls, and the floor would be strewn with *rose petals* instead of rushes.

Once Father's ship sailed, early in the spring, Mother and I set to work planning the great event.

The days passed quickly, as so often they do when one is much occupied. By the time the apples were ripe and the air was chill at night, we had already been expecting him home for some time. But the wind does its own bidding—Father had often told us so. It might blow you far off course or cease blowing altogether, leaving you stranded for weeks. Such things had happened to him before, and so we did not worry overmuch. My thoughts were still upon the wedding and how much I regretted the need to postpone it. Already there were no rose petals to be had anywhere.

Then the snow began to fall and the sewers in the road iced over, and we truly became afraid. We did not talk of it much—Mother and Alice and I—for we wished to be hopeful and keep our spirits up. But we were all plagued by the same terrible fears—except that Alice's were worse than ours, for she had seen Father's ship, and it had frightened her and given her bad dreams.

One morning there came a knock upon our door. It was gray and windy out, I remember, and we had closed all the shutters against the cold. We sat together by the fire, sewing in silence. When the rapping came, Mother did not wait for the housemaid Liddy to answer the door but leaped up with such haste that she dropped her embroidery into the coals. I quickly fished it out.

But it was not Father at the door. To our astonishment, it was Mortran Greatbeard—my Richard's father. This was most unexpected, for he had not been to our house since the days of our marriage negotiations. His manner now was exceedingly sober. I thought he seemed ill at ease.

"Madam," he said, "I have hard news for you."

# MATILDA

*T*he voyage was to have been his last. After all those years of trading in trinkets, building our fortune little by little, my husband made a bold move. He put everything we had—and still more, which he borrowed—into financing one final journey. He bought a ship and filled its hold with the very finest— *truly* the best—of paintings and wines and glassware and tapestries. These would not be traded with merchants along the coast as before. These were goods for sultans and pashas.

If all went well (and why should it not?), we would be fabulously wealthy. He would become the lord of many estates, and I his lady.

He was in high spirits when he left—hungry for the adventure, sure of his success. I think, in truth, he cared more for the triumph of his enterprise than the money and lands he would gain from it. My husband was actually *proud* that he had begun his life a poor man and had made himself a rich one. "Any fool can inherit a fortune," he liked to say. "It takes wit and hard work to make one." I thought this sentiment very odd, for to inherit wealth is *so* much more respectable. Indeed, he always was a strange man—but I would not have another.

We were accustomed to waiting, Marianne and Alice and I. Always he went away and always he came back—richer than before and bearing wonderful gifts. But we never knew when to expect him, for it is the nature of ships to be ever at the mercy of the winds.

One time he dressed himself as a peasant—dirtied his face and pulled a cowl over his head, so we would not know him—and knocked upon our door. Liddy would not allow him into the house, but did agree to "give the mistress this package."

I was busy with our accounts when she came in, most apologetically, and handed me a wad of rags, saying a filthy beggar had insisted she deliver it. I took it in my hand with some reluctance, for the cloth was soiled and reeked of garlic. But then I felt the weight of it, and became most curious, so that I began unwrapping it in haste. Inside there was a gold neck-lace—and I knew my husband was home! Ah, who-ever had such a man!

So we waited with good patience, long past the time he might be expected. Then we waited still a month more. The cold came early that year, with one storm after another moving across the land. I comforted myself by imagining that he had been forced to take shelter in some harbor along the way. But another month passed, and still he did not come. Now the snow was falling, and though I tried to train my thoughts to be hopeful, I began to fear the worst.

One morning there came a knock upon the door. I could think of nothing but that he had finally returned. I would not have Liddy delay him a moment longer, and so I ran to open it myself.

But it was not my husband. It was Mortran Greatbeard, father of Marianne's betrothed. His mien was grim, and he wasted no time on pretty words. My husband had been declared lost at sea, he said. Our creditors would demand full payment of all we owed, most likely that very day. Mortran had come to give us fair warning, for it was being much talked of all over town.

"You understand, of course," Mortran said—and I

think I saw a flash of shame cross his face as he said it—"that the arrangement between my son and your daughter is now invalid, as your circumstances have changed."

Oh, such nice wording that was—"your circumstances have changed." Meaning, of course, that we would soon lose our home, our horses, our furnishings, our dresses and jewels, the candlesticks and the saltcellar and the glassware, the bed hangings and sheets and the silver platters and the goblets and the cunning little carvings from the Far East. My husband's things, too—his books and clothes. I could not bear the thought of it!

According to the laws, our creditors should not have been allowed to take my dower lands, and that would have saved us. But no—I had been bold, too. "Borrow against my dower lands," I had said. "The more you have to spend on cargo, the greater the riches in the end!"

Now the greater the ruin.

Mortran, having said his piece, bowed curtly to us all and left. Marianne managed to keep her composure until the door was shut, then ran screaming to her chamber. I did not go after her, for my legs were trembling, and I felt so light-headed I feared I might faint. I went over and sat down on the bench beside Alice, though she seemed not to notice I was there.

She sat, unmoving, her hands crossed over her lips and her eyes very wide.

"Mistress?" It was Liddy. I had not heard her approach, and so her voice startled me. "Mistress," she said again, "pardon that I overheard."

"So then you know everything," I said, not turning to look at her, but staring dejectedly into the fire. "That is just as well. I will pay your wages now, while I still have something left. Obviously, then, you must go. Cook, too. All of you."

"But Mistress," she said, "just a little thought . . ."

I turned around now. She was wringing her hands nervously, but her face was eager.

"Do they know—do your creditors know *everything* you have? Every dress, every silk shawl or ivory comb?"

"Well . . . ," I said, trying to imagine what path her thoughts were taking. "Not *every single thing* in this house is itemized. Only those things of greatest value."

"So then, that's good."

"Liddy, please make your point."

"I will, Mistress. See, when I go home in the evenings, from time to time I take a basket of stale bread or the like. It is common practice enough." I had long suspected that more than stale bread went home with Liddy, but I was prepared to hear her out.

"So what if, instead, I took home a few gold bracelets or silver spoons or a diamond clasp? Whatever would fit in a basket and isn't—what's the word? *Itemized?* And then after all the wicked men have come and took all you have, why then you come by my house and pick them up. They'd be none the wiser, now, would they? And you'd have a bit of *seed money* so to speak—to start over with. You might reward me in some small way, I'd think, for doing you that little service?"

Then she folded her arms and smiled and waited for my reaction.

# MARIANNE

*W*as it not hard enough already that Father was dead and we were ruined? Must we also have old garlic-breathed Mortran Greatbeard come to our house and announce that he would not allow that pimple-faced, pig-eyed son of his to marry me, now that I am penniless?

One minute I was about to be wed in grand style to a wealthy man—then suddenly I am rejected, thrown onto the ash heap, into the gutter—no longer good enough for toothless, dim-witted Richard! Oh, it was too much! Can you wonder that I took to my bed and wept over it? Was that not the *natural* thing to do?

Well, Mother did not seem to think so, for she proceeded to give me a tongue-lashing over it, demanding I control myself and attend to the matter at hand. Oh, how she prattled on, till I thought I would *scream*, saying we must "rise to the occasion" and "control our own destiny" and many other such commonplace remarks. She must be made of ice, that woman, that she could be so sensible, with Father dead and my engagement broken!

My sister, Alice, did not "rise to the occasion," either—she just sat there upon the bench as still as a stone, and did not utter a single word after smelly old Crumbs-in-His-Greatbeard left our house. Mother seemed to find Alice's silence just as annoying as my wails and moans. She slapped my sister on the cheek to get her to stop sulking. Then she slapped me, too.

And so we had little choice but to set our grief aside and go help Mother find as many small, precious things as we could, so that Liddy might carry them away from the house before the creditors came. And I must admit, it was a good plan. Not two hours later a pair of grim-faced men arrived at our door— just as flatulent old Mortran Grossbelly said they might.

Mother had told us to change into our finest gowns before the creditors came. This was not a matter of pride. She said they were bound to take our jewels—but she was sure they would never stoop so low as to strip us of our dresses and send us naked into the street. Nor did she think they would have the nerve to tear the seed pearls from my bodice or cut the marten collar off her mantle. So why not let them take the everyday gowns and walk out in our best?

Of course, they were not fooled by this strategy. "You count upon our chivalry, I see," said one, lowering his eyelids in a suggestive manner. I will not repeat what the other man said, for it was most offensive and very cruel.

On the whole they were a vile, coldhearted pair. They did not seem the least bit sorry for us. They rejoiced over our beautiful things most shamelessly, as though we were not standing right there to hear every word they said. It revolted me to see them pawing through our treasures with their coarse, dirty hands and sitting in the very chair where once my father sat! Oh, it was horrible!

But we did not have to endure their company for long. Once the contents of our house and stable were inspected and all the papers signed, they turned us out.

It was a cold day, but shutters were open all along the street. I saw the faces of our neighbors peering down at us from their windows. Not one of them thought to offer us shelter, or even bothered to come out and tell us good-bye. How that chilled me! I had thought them our friends. I had planned to invite those people to my wedding!

I looked back only once, but then I began to weep again and Mother took firm hold of my arm. "Be as dignified as you can, Marianne," she said. "Hold your head high and walk away like the lady you are."

And so we did. Dressed in our finest gowns and wearing our stylish little pointed shoes, we paraded out of that lovely neighborhood and headed for the working-class district where Liddy dwelt. Mother said we would find a room to rent there, something clean but modest. Then, once she had collected our trinkets and sold a few, we would find something better.

I noticed, as we made our way, how the buildings grew ever shabbier and the lanes narrower and more crowded. There was a ripe smell of filth in the air. These common folk emptied their chamber pots right outside their doors, each house with its own revolting little pile! And the people were vulgar and discourteous; they pushed and shoved us as we walked and shouted at us to get out of the way of carts and horses.

Though we took great care not to walk in the gutters and navigated as best we could around horse droppings and garbage and other refuse, still our shoes were soon wet and stained. Nor was it easy to walk on cobblestones in those dainty slippers. Twice I turned my ankles, and was soon hobbling along like a cripple.

As the afternoon wore on, it became clear that finding "clean but modest" lodgings would not be as easy as Mother had imagined. People were suspicious of us—three ladies dressed so grandly, inquiring after a furnished room in such a humble part of town. Who were we? Trollops? Thieves? Certainly, they did not want the likes of *us* living in their God-fearing houses!

By the time the curfew bell rang for closing time, matters were desperate. It was growing colder, and we were hungry and exhausted. Though I knew Mother would scold me for weeping, I could not help it. I feared we would have to sleep out on the street!

Seeing how things were, Mother entered a nearby tavern. It did not meet her standards of "clean but modest"; indeed, she would never have set foot in such a place had we not been so very wretched. But a boy selling meat pies said he thought room and board might be had there, though he did not know the price.

I felt a stab of hope when I saw the proprietress. She was a bit unkempt, but she had a kindly face. And she showed she had a good heart, too, when Mother told her the truth: that we were ladies of high estate who had been thrown into poverty of a sudden, and had no protector. Our fine clothes were all we had in the world—those and a few trinkets. All we asked was a roof, a bed, and a meal.

She looked at me, my face still wet with tears, then at Alice, who stood there trembling with cold and numb with sorrow. Then she looked at Mother with genuine sympathy and said she would take us in.

She gave us a room near the kitchen. It was dirty, and it smelled of fish and onions. Instead of the featherbeds with silk hangings we were accustomed to, we would have to sleep on a single straw pallet upon the floor—no doubt infested with fleas or lice. It was most disgustingly stained, too, and there were no bedclothes and no blanket. All else the room contained were two stools, a cracked chamber pot, and a tiny window with no glass and a broken shutter. This was to be our home for the night.

As it was growing dark, Mother hurried off to find Liddy while the landlady led Alice and me into the kitchen for some supper (she did not think it proper for us to eat in the main hall of the tavern with all those rowdy men).

She gave us each a thick slice of coarse brown bread and a tankard of watery ale. Peasant fare. I turned to Alice to see if she found it as revolting as I did, but she only stared at her meal, insensible, as though she had never seen bread before.

"I fear we must eat it, Alice," I said, in a low voice

so the landlady would not hear, "for there is nothing better to be had." She looked up at me with puppy eyes, then down again. At last she picked up her bread and began nibbling at it distractedly.

As for me, I ate every crumb of mine, for all that it was dry and stale. And though the ale was thin and bitter, I drank every drop. Then, when we were finished, I took Alice by the hand and we went upstairs to our ugly little room to wait for Mother.

# ALICE

*I* sat on one stool and Marianne sat on the other, waiting. There was naught to do in that room, and there was no candle, so it soon grew dark in there. The only light came through the broken part of the shutter, but it brought us little comfort.

I wanted to sleep more than anything in the world, but I could not bear to lie down upon that pallet with its horrid stains and smell of mildew. I would have slept more readily upon the floor, but it was even dirtier and would have ruined my gown (it was too cold to take it off). Marianne seemed to feel much the same, though we did not speak of it. She sat in her corner; I sat in mine.

Mother was gone a long time. We heard the bell ring for Compline. The streets were quiet and the moon was already rising over the rooftops—yet still she did not come. I began to feel light-headed with fear and had to tell myself to take slow, deep breaths, sitting there on my hard little stool and leaning back against the wall. Mother would be back soon. Perhaps she had already returned and had only stopped downstairs to have something to eat. It calmed me somewhat to imagine it.

At last I heard the welcome sound of footsteps in the hall. The door opened, slowly and quietly; she must have thought we were asleep. Dark though it was, I could see she was carrying something in her arms.

"Mother?" cried Marianne, leaping from her stool. She sounded as frightened as I was.

"Yes," Mother said. "Where are you, Marianne? It's hard to see."

"I'm here. Alice is over in the corner, on the other stool. We did not like to lie upon that bed."

"I know," Mother said, "but you cannot sit up all night. Here, I have a bedsheet and a blanket from the landlady. They will have to do for tonight. Tomorrow we will leave, first thing."

She spread the sheet over the pallet and tucked it in.

"Now let me help you take your dresses off," she said then. "You must fold them carefully and lay them on the stools so they do not get any more soiled than they already are." She found us in the dark and helped us undress. I could tell that something was wrong.

"Mother, do you have the basket?" Marianne asked.

"Get under the covers and we shall talk about it," Mother said. "Hurry, children, or you will catch a chill!"

We did as we were told. I could smell the mildew through the sheet, and the blanket was coarse and scratchy, but it was warm. Marianne lay on one side of Mother and I on the other. We huddled together like three kittens in a basket.

"Now tell us!" Marianne said.

"As you wish," Mother answered with a sigh, "though you will not like what I have to say. I did *not* get the basket, Marianne. Those directions Liddy gave me to her house—which I wrote down so carefully on parchment and secreted in my bodice—were false. There was no such street in that quarter, no such bakeshop on the corner. Alas, Liddy was cleverer than I took her for. I had thought to give her my green shawl as a reward—but instead, she has taken it all. We were outfoxed by a housemaid—think of that!"

She let us weep for a while, and then shushed us.

"That's enough, children," she said. "Tears cannot help us now. I have been thinking hard upon the matter and have formed a new plan. Much as I do not like to do it, we must go to my sister's house. She will not like it, either, but she will take us in."

"But your sister lives far away," I said.

"Yes—in the King's City. We can walk there in a week, I would guess."

"Walk!" cried Marianne. "For a week?"

"Oh, Mother, no!" I cried. "We cannot go away! How will Father find us?"

"He won't need to find us, you little dunce," said Marianne. "He's dead! Can't you get that through your thick skull?"

"Stop it," Mother hissed, "both of you! I am no happier about this than you are, but we must do something; we must turn to someone. I would much rather go to my brother, if you would know the truth, but his lands are too far to the north. My sister it must be, then."

"But what about Father?" I whimpered.

"I will send a message to the ship chandler at the port. If God has spared your father's life and he should someday return, then he will learn soon enough where to find us. But Alice, child—your dreams are telling you what your heart does not wish to accept. He is lost to us, and that must be the end of it."

"No!" I cried, clinging to Mother so hard I nearly choked her.

"Stop it, Alice!" She was exasperated. "This is not the time to give way. We must be strong. Now quit your whimpering, both of you, and listen. Tomorrow I will sell my mantle—the fur collar should bring a good price. I will buy something plain but warm to wear in its stead. And some stout shoes for us to walk in. When we arrive at my sister's, we will put the fine ones on again. I do not wish to make a pitiful display at her door."

"Is she terribly grand, then—your sister?" Marianne asked.

"She is now. She wasn't always."

"You don't like her, do you?" I said.

"No. We were never close, and then we had a falling out. When I married your father, Basilia remarked that I was marrying below my station for money. I replied that she had married *above* her station for nothing. And that was true at the time—her husband, Lord Percy, was a second son with only a small holding. But he was lucky in war and came home with cartloads of booty, and then he did the crown prince a service on a battlefield in Brutanna and was rewarded handsomely by the king. Now my sister has connections at court and a splendid house. She has far eclipsed our life at its grandest. She will enjoy my downfall, I'm afraid. It won't be pleasant. But her beds will be clean, I can promise you that."

We were silent for a long time. I thought the others had fallen asleep, but then Marianne asked softly, "Mother, might your sister find *me* a place at court, do you think?"

"Shh," Mother said. "Who knows?"

When their breathing at last grew deep and slow and had not altered for some minutes, I wiggled away from the warmth of Mother's body and the coarse comfort of the blanket. I stood silently for a moment, barefoot and shivering, listening for signs that I had awakened them, but Mother and Marianne slept on.

And so I tiptoed over to the stool where my dress lay and, with my fingers, followed the folds of the skirt down to the hem. It was still damp from the road, and it sickened me to imagine what manner of foul wetness I might be touching. But touch it I must, for I had hidden something precious there, and now I must find it.

Carefully I worked my fingers along the hem until I felt a lump. Then all that remained was to slide it to the spot in the back of the gown where the stitches were more widely spaced, and pull it out—my beautiful emerald ring.

Father had given it to me some years before. He said the sultan of Arabia had sent it, having heard such reports of my beauty that he had fallen in love with me and wished to shower me with riches. I told Father I didn't believe him, that he was only telling tales. But he said, "No, Alice, it is a magical ring — look into the emerald and you can see the sultan watching you."

So I did look — and to my amazement, I *could* see a face there, when the light struck the stone in just the right way. So from that time on it became our little game, Father's and mine. He would ask me what the sultan was doing that day, and I would make things up about how he was sitting in a corner weeping because he could not have me for his harem (in truth, the sultan appeared to be busy with ordinary affairs and did not seem to be pining for me at all).

When Father left on his last voyage, he told me that any time I was missing him too badly, I could always look for him in the ring. It wasn't only the sultan in there, he said. I could look for whomever I wanted. And so, one summer day when Father was more than usually in my thoughts, I took the ring out of the chest where I kept it and held it to the light. And truly his face *was* there, deep in the green of the stone. He was smiling. He winked at me!

Later, when the first cold winds of autumn arrived and Father had not yet returned, I took the ring out again. Only now the emerald had grown cloudy. I could still see Father's face in it, but not so well as before; the image came and went as if lit by a flickering candle. And Father was no longer smiling, but appeared frightened and agitated. He seemed to be shouting, or perhaps he was screaming—only I could not hear him, of course.

That vision had disturbed me so that I put the ring away and had not looked at it since—not until Mortran Greatbeard came, bearing his terrible news. When Mother told us to gather up small, precious things to send away with Liddy, I could not bring myself to trust the ring to her. Nor was I willing to leave it in my trunk for the creditors to carry away. And so I sewed it into the hem of my gown. I did not have the time then—or the courage—to look into the emerald.

But I would do it now, for I *must* know if Father still lived. And so I went over to the window and opened the shutter a crack. The moon was but a quarter full; only a thin shaft of cold, blue light streamed into the room. Carefully I angled the ring so that the moonlight pierced the emerald. And what I saw there made me gasp and tremble so that I almost dropped the ring, for it was the same terrible image that had come to me, night after night, in my dreams.

And it was then I knew that Father was never coming back.

# MATILDA

*L*ord Percy's house was grand and impos-
ing—four stories high, with leaded glass
in every window. Above the magnificent
double doors—gleaming mahogany, they
were, and enormous—the Percy coat of arms
was carved into the lintel. My sister's husband
had indeed risen in the world! How Basilia
was going to enjoy lording it over me. And
how I wished we had some other place to go!
But as we did not, I took a deep breath and
knocked upon the door.

The maid who answered left us standing
upon the stoop while she went to report our
arrival to my sister. I suspect Basilia kept us
waiting still longer out of malice. But at last

she came out to greet us.

"Why, *Matilda!*" she chirped. "Is that *you*? How *unexpected!*"

She shepherded us off the stoop and into the anteroom. And there we stood, as though my sister believed we had only just dropped by and would be leaving soon.

"Do you think we might go upstairs, Basilia—to the great hall?" I asked. "I have hard news to tell you and would find it somewhat easier if I could at least sit down."

"As you wish," she said, then turned and ascended the stairs—quite grandly and in no particular hurry. I assumed we were meant to follow.

Once we were settled before the fire, Basilia folded her hands and batted her eyes and tilted her head in her most artificial semblance of politeness. "What brings you here, sister?" she asked.

"Calamity," I replied bluntly.

"*Indeed?*"

"Indeed," I said. "My husband has perished at sea."

Basilia seemed genuinely taken aback by this and said she was very sorry to hear it. Then, after a respectable pause, she asked what business had brought us to the city at such a time. Would we not grieve more comfortably at home? As she spoke, I saw her glancing at my gown—mud-spattered and torn from our journey—then at Marianne's ruined slippers. Her eyes finally rested on poor Alice, who sat in grim and stony silence, her pale skin ghostly in the firelight.

"We have lost everything," I said simply, "and have come here because we have nowhere else to go."

Basilia showed great amazement. She leaned forward. She wanted to hear more! Question followed question until she had unearthed every painful detail of our financial ruin, our eviction, and the terrible journey that had brought us to her door. Humiliation, it seemed, was to be the price of my sister's charity.

When I had finished my story, I waited for her response. She pinched her lips and rolled her eyes upward as if to ask advice from the roof beams. She made nervous sniffling noises. Then at last she came to a decision: she would have to confer with her husband, Lord Percy, before committing to anything of a permanent nature, she said. But as he was away just then on the king's business, and as we were destitute and homeless, and as the honor of the family demanded it—in a word, we were welcome to stay in her house "for a time."

Then, as though she had not mortified us enough already, Basilia asked if we would like to bathe (lowering her eyes demurely as if to spare us any embarrassment) and change into "something a bit less travel worn." She knew perfectly well that we had brought no other clothes, but she made me say it. Then she pretended to be much surprised and offered us some of her cast-off gowns. All in all, I must say I endured my sister's condescension with remarkable composure.

Lord Percy was away for more than a week. During that time, Marianne quickly recovered her spirits. She was clearly at ease in my sister's grand house, and while she had the grace and wit to compliment Basilia from time to time on some fine ornament or dainty dish, Marianne was never fawning or subservient. She showed the confidence of the beautiful, well-bred girl she was—a young lady with refined tastes and elegant manners, very much accustomed to luxury.

To my surprise, Basilia took notice of these qualities and began to seek my daughter out. Marianne was invited to play backgammon with her. Marianne's opinion was sought on the matter of which necklace Basilia ought to wear. I understood from this that my childless sister was lonely and that my clever daughter saw an advantage and took it.

One day Marianne emerged from Basilia's chamber wearing a dress of fine-spun wool, green to match her eyes. That evening at dinner she wore pearls about her neck. And though my sister did not extend her generosity to Alice and me, she seemed to soften toward us, simply because of our relation to Marianne. And for that, at least, I was grateful.

This was the state of things when Lord Percy finally came home.

"Sister-in-law!" he said in greeting as he strode into the hall. "What a surprise!"

I would not have recognized him. The proud and petulant boy who had married my sister had matured into a gruff and impatient, bearlike man, keenly aware of his own importance and accustomed to giving orders.

"Why is she here?" he asked Basilia in a booming voice. He took off his heavy, fur-lined mantle and handed it to his wife, who handed it to a servant. Lord Percy did not bother with courtesy because he did not have to.

"Perhaps you would prefer to discuss the matter in private?" I suggested. And as neither of them urged me to stay, I curtsied politely and retired to the little room I shared with Marianne and Alice. It was nearly dark by the time a servant came to summon us into the great hall.

We found my sister and her husband comfortably seated before the fire in large chairs of intricately carved oak with high backs and velvet cushions. Lord

Percy indicated a bench where we were to sit.

"Basilia tells me that you are now a widow, and penniless besides," he began.

"Yes," I said, "that is true."

"Most regrettable."

I agreed that it was.

Lord Percy now turned his attention to Marianne. "My wife is of the opinion that you might do well at court. She speaks highly of your manners and taste and so on—and at first glance, I am inclined to agree with her. I will recommend you to Prince Gilbert, for his wife has recently lost one of her ladies-in-waiting—"

"Yes, poor Gwendolyn!" Basilia interrupted. "She succumbed to an ailment of the chest."

Lord Percy glared daggers at his wife, who promptly closed her mouth and looked down at her feet.

"You will need decent clothes. Basilia will see to that and will allow you to wear some of her jewels, so that you will make a proper impression. In such circles there is perhaps a chance you may even make a good marriage. Though you have no money, the connection with my family might be incentive enough for some ambitious young man. And you are pretty enough, I'll grant."

"Oh, thank you, Lord Percy!" Marianne said,

positively aglow at the prospect of life at court.

Now the great man turned his attention back to me. "Is it true, Matilda, that your husband squandered not only his own money, but your dower lands as well?"

"I borrowed against my dower lands quite freely and with my whole heart. We stood to make an immense fortune."

"Then you were a fool," Lord Percy said. "And you have ruined yourself, for you will not easily find another husband without money or property."

"I had not thought to marry again," I said.

"Well you *must* think of it. You have no alternative. And furthermore, you cannot afford to be too particular in the matter." He was looking me over as if I were a horse he might want to buy. "You are handsome enough for a woman of your age," he conceded, "and a knight's daughter, and sister to my wife. Perhaps some man will be fool enough to take you for that alone."

"You are too kind," I said drily.

"I am not kind at all," he answered, "but I *will* endeavor to find you a husband, which is of more use to you than sweet words."

He looked at Alice then, but spoke to me. "The child is mute?" he asked.

"The child has lost her father. She loved him

dearly, and grief has troubled her mind. She will mend in time."

"Nevertheless, she is an encumbrance. A penniless widow is bad enough. A penniless widow with a mute child is worse."

"*Perhaps*," I said, through clenched teeth, "you can find me a man who *does not like noise*."

At this, Lord Percy leaned his head back and laughed. "Yes, Matilda," he said, "perhaps I can!"

# BOOK THREE

## The Slippers of Glass

# MARIANNE

*L*ord Percy was as good as his word. Before the month was out, he had found me a place at court—and as lady-in-waiting to a princess, too! I could scarcely believe my good fortune!

Of course, Princess Alana was only the wife of the king's *second* son, Gilbert, and so she would never be the queen. This *was* something of a disappointment to me, if truth be told. Oh, I do not mean to sound ungrateful. It is a great honor—an incredible privilege—to serve in the household of a princess, *any* princess, no matter how lowly. And though it would have been so much grander to have served Princess Berta, still, I did not complain.

But then—oh, what an amazing series of events transpired! First King Raymond was struck down by the fever. Then the crown prince fell ill also, and followed his father in death only three days after. And thus, quite unexpectedly, Prince Gilbert assumed the throne—and as I served his wife, I became handmaid to the *queen of Moranmoor*! Imagine!

Naturally, I was as sorry as everyone else that King Raymond and Prince John died. It was such a terrible loss to the kingdom! Still, as the poet said, it is an ill wind that turns none to good. And certainly it was good for me, the way things turned out.

I think sometimes of our neighbors back home, and how cruelly they treated us in our time of distress. I wish they could see me now. They would be sick with envy. And heartily sorry, too, that they did not treat me more kindly while they had the chance.

I think of Father, also, almost every day, and how he would rejoice at my success! I picture him looking down on me from heaven and pointing me out to the other angels: "Look! See there, in the palace of Moranmoor—the beautiful young lady arranging the queen's hair? *That* is my daughter Marianne!" Oh, he would be so happy for me!

I only wish the same could be said of Mother and Alice. If Father knew what had become of *them*, it would break his heart.

Mother had no choice but to marry again, you see, penniless and cast adrift as she was. And so once again, Lord Percy kept his word. He found her a husband, a widower of good birth and some fortune. Now my mother dwells in this man's house, a knight by the name of Edward, and he is as cold and stern as Father was warmhearted and amiable. I consider myself fortunate twice over that I am so much at court and need rarely be at home.

Mother was not married to Edward for many months—and bitter months they were, too, with him expecting her to make order in a household that had been in disarray since the death of his first wife—when he announced that he had a daughter by that marriage and that she would soon be coming to live with them. This daughter had been living among *peasants* all her life!

Imagine it, then, if you will: it is late afternoon. Edward is alone in the solar, the sunny upstairs room where he sits for hours with his books; Mother and Alice are in the great hall, busy with their needlework. I am visiting for a few days and, as they sew, I am regaling them with stories of life at court. (Poor Alice does not join in these conversations, for she is as dumb as a stone, her mind much disordered since Father died.)

There comes a knock at the door, and a few

moments later the housemaid ushers in as ridiculous a pair as you might ever hope to see. The first is a plump lady of middle age wearing an idiotic grin and a gown of questionable taste—the sort of thing a butcher's wife might think very elegant. Her wimple is askew. Beside her stands a girl of about Alice's age, wearing some shabby garment of olive wool, a black winter cap covering her head and ears, and mud-caked, round-toed shoes of coarse leather. This peasant attire is made all the more ridiculous by the overlong scarlet mantle she wears, for it is of fine cloth and lined with fur, clearly belonging to somebody else.

Her face, I confess, might be thought handsome were her skin not so dirty and sun-browned and did she not possess those startling eyebrows of a carroty hue—never *once* plucked in all her life—setting off such a pair of piercing blue eyes.

These two outlandish figures proved, once introductions had been made, to be Maud, the sister of Edward's first wife, and our new stepsister, Isabel.

Mother sent the maid up to the solar to fetch Edward, who quickly sent the sister-in-law packing—rather rudely, I thought, considering their former connection and the fact that she had traveled some great distance (at his request) to bring his daughter home.

Once Maud had departed (after first kissing Isabel

many times, and embracing her, and weeping copious tears at their parting), Edward studied the girl silently for a good long time.

"*Isabel*, is it?" he said at last.

"Yes, Father." She curtsied awkwardly.

"Take off the cap," he said. She did so.

"You do resemble your mother somewhat," he said, "though her hair was more of gold than brass. Perhaps yours will be more golden once it is clean." He turned to Mother then. "She needs a good washing—and some respectable clothes."

"If you will recommend a dressmaker, I will summon her right away," Mother said.

"A *dressmaker*? When you have nothing to do all day but ply your needle? Do not put on airs, Matilda. Just wash the child—she stinks, and most likely she is crawling with vermin. And if you cannot make her a gown yourself, then give her something of Alice's."

"*Wash* her?" Mother gasped, appalled. "You want *me* to *wash* her?"

"Just see that it is done, Matilda—you can manage that much, I think. Chances are she can wash herself, though I doubt she has had much practice at it. And when she is clean and properly dressed, bring her back to me and we shall see whether she truly resembles Catherine or no."

Mother turned on her heel and stormed out of the

hall; Alice and Isabel and I followed quickly after. "He is a monster!" she muttered.

We went straight to the kitchen, where Mother ordered the scullery maid to heat some water for a bath and told Isabel to stay there till it was ready. "Can I assume that you will know what to do with it?" Mother asked.

Isabel flushed and said she would.

Then we left the kitchen and Mother—still in a fury—went tearing through the house, rummaging through chests and drawers in search of *something* to put on the girl. Finally, in the storeroom, in a chest of cypress wood, Mother found some ladies' clothes and shoes and under-linen, all carefully folded away with a scattering of bay leaves between each layer to keep them sweet. She took out a gown of fine wool in a deep indigo color, trimmed with ermine.

"Oh—how elegant!" I said. "Whose do you think it was?"

"His late wife's, I suppose, or perhaps his mother's. Edward might even have had a sister—I would certainly be the last to know of it. I do not rightly care, Marianne, if you would know the truth."

"But isn't that much too grand for little ash-face?"

"Have you a better idea, Marianne?" she snapped back. "Would you have her wear something of Alice's—or of yours?"

It was not a real question. She already knew the answer.

By the time we returned to the kitchen, the maid was busy tossing buckets of dirty bathwater out the window into the street, and Isabel was sitting by the fire, drying her hair. Her skin was an entire shade lighter, I noticed.

"When you are dry, put this on. If it does not fit, then we shall have to see what we can do to alter it."

"I can sew, my lady," Isabel said. "Whatever is needed, I can do it."

"Well, that is a relief," Mother said. "But you must not say 'my lady.' You are a knight's daughter, and you must learn to behave like one."

"How shall I address you, then?"

Mother paused to think. "Stepmother, I suppose," she said.

Then we went to sit in the great hall and wait until Isabel was dry and dressed and ready to be presented to Edward a second time. Alice retreated to our room, as she so often did. Mother took up her work again, still much agitated, jabbing her needle into the embroidery with savage force. We sat in silence for a while, irritation filling the air like an evil smell. Then suddenly I thought of something.

"Mother," I said, "where is Isabel to sleep?"

She laid her sewing in her lap and looked up at me,

aghast. She had not yet considered this. "Oh, dear child!" she said. "She must sleep with you and Alice—there is nowhere else."

"Oh, Mother, no! He cannot make me share a bed with that dirty peasant!"

"Then you may return to court early, Marianne. You are most fortunate that you have that choice. But what of poor Alice? Troubled as she is, I cannot bear to think of her lying beside that strange child at night."

"Let ash-face sleep in the kitchen, then—that is what she is accustomed to."

"Marianne, you make me weary sometimes," Mother said. "I am trying to think." She returned to attacking her embroidery with her needle while I gazed at the fire.

Not long thereafter Isabel came into the hall dressed in the blue gown, her hair combed and lying free upon her shoulders. Her cheeks were bright, and she smelled of soap. The gown was a bit loose about the bodice, but it would do well enough. Indeed, such was the transformation that one might almost have taken her for a lady—were it not for the awkward way she walked in her dainty little shoes.

"Excellent," Mother said, rising from her chair. "You are much improved, Isabel. Let us take you to your father for inspection."

"Oh, Stepmother," Isabel said, "it is such a beautiful

gown! Like the sky on a clear night."

"Just so," Mother said. "Now come along."

And so we led Isabel up to the solar and presented her to Edward.

"Here is your daughter, husband," Mother said, "washed and dressed as you requested."

But he did not smile, nor did he compliment us on the transformation. He rose to his feet, unmindful that his book fell onto the floor. Indeed, he trampled upon it as he strode across the room, roaring like a wild beast. His dark eyes were fierce with rage.

"How *dare* you!" he shouted, grabbing Mother fiercely by the arm. "Is this your idea of a *jest*, woman?" Then he slapped her face. I gasped and clung to the doorframe, knowing not whether to run or stay.

Then he turned on Isabel. "Take it off!" he said in a low growl.

"Here? Now?" said Isabel, retreating toward the door. She clearly knew not what to do—did he expect her to stand before us in her *underclothes*?

"Take it *off*, I say!" and he began pulling and tugging at the dress until it ripped at the neckline and along the right sleeve.

Isabel turned and fled from him, struggling with the buttons as she went, crying, "I am taking it off! I am taking it off!"

At the bottom of the stairs, she finally freed herself from the lovely blue dress that had reminded her of the night sky. She left it lying there and disappeared.

"Have you gone *mad*?" Mother cried, her hand against her burning cheek.

"No, Matilda, not mad. But I fear you shall drive me to it. On whose authority did you go into my dead wife's chest and dress that child like a ghost out of the past? Tell me!"

"I did not think it mattered *whose* dress it was," Mother said. "I thought only to do as you commanded and find her something to wear. And since my reward was a slap in the face, you may dress your daughter however you please, but do not come to *me* about it."

The rage was out of him now.

"Go," he said.

"And gladly," she snapped back.

Mother slept that night with Alice and me, while Isabel slept in the kitchen. When I saw little ash-face at breakfast the next morning, she was once again dressed in her old peasant gown of olive wool. And as neither Mother nor Edward seemed willing to do aught about it, she went on wearing it from that day on. It was enough to put you off your food!

As you might imagine, I was heartily glad to pack my things that very day and return to court!

# BELLA

*I* did not like it in that house. No one was happy there.

Not my father, who prowled the halls like a caged beast, haunted by ghosts and poisoned by grief. He scarcely spoke to me, except to criticize. I often wondered why he brought me home at all, unless it was so he might stare at me endlessly, searching my face for the living shadow of my long-dead mother.

Nor was my stepmother happy, for she had been forced to marry a man who was not amiable in the least and who regarded her with contempt. She had one daughter who could not speak and another who thought only of herself. And then she had *me* thrust upon her, quite unexpected and very much unwanted—a coarse and ignorant bumpkin who sat in her hall every day, reminding her always of that first marriage and that first wife whom her husband seemed unable to forget.

And most certainly Alice was not happy, for she had crept into the darkness and dwelt there, overcome by silent grief.

I believe the very mice in the baseboards and the fleas among the rushes were unhappy there. Misery filled the house like a fog, seeping into every corner, chilling us on the warmest days, robbing the finest food of its savor. However white the bread or spiced the wine, all tasted flat when eaten at their table.

There seemed no proper place for me in that household, unless it was to be stared at by Father and scolded by Stepmother and mocked by Marianne and ignored by Alice. I think at first they had some intentions of improving me, so that I might be decently married off as soon as possible. But they quickly lost interest in the project, or were discouraged by the hopelessness of it. Whichever it was, they taught me precious little of how a lady ought to behave, unless you count such rebukes as, "Do not eat like a *ploughman*, Isabel!" or "Are you a hunchback, child? Sit up straight!"

As they seemed not to know what to do with me, and as it was plain they found my presence bothersome, I took to spending my time in the kitchen. It was warm and the air smelled of roasting pig and onions, cinnamon and rosemary. There was work for me to do, and laughter. Cook called me a "right jolly lass" and patted my cheek and smiled at me. (She did not have to live in that house all the time and so had not succumbed to the gloom of the place.)

I think she was glad of my help, for the kitchen maid was lazy and none too bright, whereas I was eager to help and already knew much of cookery. I could roast meat and brew ale and make eel pie and other such common fare, though I knew naught of fancy dishes. At the cottage we had never made dainties like bone-marrow pie, with its many layers of marrow mixed with currants, artichoke souls, great raisins, damson prunes, cinnamon, dates, and rosewater. Cook got the receipt out of a little book she had. I asked her if we might make more of those dishes, so that I could learn how to prepare them.

"Why, of course," she said, and squeezed my hand. "Just look through the book and tell me what you fancy."

"I cannot," I said, "for I never learned my letters."

"Well, then, we'll go over them together, won't we? I'm no great reader myself, but I can usually make out such words as are in the receipts." (She only said this to be kind—she could read perfectly well, and I knew it.)

After that, whenever time allowed, Cook would tell me the names of the various receipts, and we would choose one of them to make the following day. I enjoyed this, and I think she did, too; it made her work less monotonous. Even Stepmother commented on it, saying our meals had become more varied and interesting of late, not just the same old roast meats day after day. I tried hard not to smile when I heard her say this. Had she known I had aught to do with it, she would have found fault with every dish.

One morning Cook and I set out to make a salmon and fruit tart. As I had made pastry many a time in the old days, she set me to doing that while she simmered the fruits in wine—figs, dates, raisins, and currants—and cut up the fish. Once I had made the pastry coffin, she would show me how to fill it with layers of fish, fruits, spices, and pine nuts—that way I would remember how to do it the next time.

I was standing at the kitchen table, kneading the dough and watching Cook at her preparations, when suddenly the door swung open and Stepmother came in. This startled me, for Stepmother *never* came into the kitchen. She preferred to summon Cook out to the great hall if there was anything she needed to discuss with her.

Whatever had brought her there, she was about to

say something to Cook when, out of the corner of her eye, she spotted me. All was quiet for a moment. Then Stepmother turned her head in a slow and affected manner and fixed me with a hard, cold stare. This made me most uneasy—just as it was meant to do. My hands began to tremble, and I grew breathless and light-headed. It was then, as I took a step back from the table to make sure of my balance, that I dropped the pastry onto the floor!

Cook gasped, the kitchen maid squealed, and all eyes gazed down to where the pastry lay at my feet. "Oh!" I cried, retrieving the ruined dough and stupidly making as if to brush it off.

"Well, Isabel," Stepmother said, "I see you are just as inept in the kitchen as you are everywhere else."

"Oh, Madam," Cook said most anxiously, "I hope you do not mind that I let her help in the kitchen sometimes. I just thought—even a highborn lady needs to know *somewhat* of cookery."

Stepmother sighed expressively and closed her eyes to show her impatience. "Highborn she may be, Cook," she said, "but a lady—never! If you can teach her anything at all, then I will be glad of it. You are welcome to her."

Cook's face brightened. "Oh, thank you, Madam!" she gushed. "Indeed, Miss Isabel is a most clever—"

"There will be five of us for dinner, all this week,"

Stepmother said, clearly not wishing to hear of my cleverness. "Miss Marianne is coming home from court."

"Yes, Madam," Cook said with a curtsy and a nod, "I will take note of it."

Then Stepmother looked over to where I stood, still holding my sad little lump of dirty pastry, and said, "Make sure you throw that out." And then she left.

I was too disheartened after that to help Cook with the pie. I went over and sat in the corner. It was all I could do to keep from weeping.

I had never asked to come live there. I would rather have stayed in the village, where I was happy, for all that it was so humble. But as it seemed that I had no choice but to live in my father's house, I had done my best to please him and my stepmother. I tried always to be pleasant and helpful. I minded my manners and spoke softly and absented myself whenever I seemed to be in the way. Whatever they bid me do, I did it eagerly. But none of this did any good. Clearly I was still an annoyance to them. What little time we spent together—at meals, and on occasion in the great hall—was painful for everybody.

Why, then, did they not just marry me off and be rid of me? Because I was too coarse and stupid to make a decent match, that's why. And besides, if they were unwilling to give me a respectable dress, such as a knight's daughter ought to wear (neither Father nor Stepmother would submit in the matter, after their loathsome quarrel), what were the chances they would provide me with a dowry sufficient to buy me a suitor? No, like as not, I would grow old in that dismal house, unwanted and unloved.

While I was engaged in these bleak musings, my fingers had been busy playing with the dough, pinching off bits of it and forming them into little animals. And, indeed, I was rather pleased by the results—for you could easily tell which were the sheep and which the cows. I showed them to Cook, and she smiled.

"What a clever lass you are!" she said. "Why don't you set them in the oven this afternoon, once the fire is out? They will dry nice and hard and then you can keep them, you see. I will show you how, before I go."

Her kindness lifted my spirits, and I decided I would give her one or two of the animals, for she had been good to me, and she seemed to fancy them.

Working with my hands has always calmed me, and it did so now. As I sat there, shaping the little legs of another cow and forming its head and giving it a set of delicate horns and a slender rope of a tail, my mind carried me out of the kitchen and back to the village where I had been a child—where life had been simple, and I was loved and felt safe.

I put the little cow aside and began, very carefully,

to shape the figure of a lady. I gave her a simple gown, and an apron, and a headdress such as Mother always wore. I took a broom straw and used it to poke two holes for eyes and draw a delicate line for a mouth. Then I pinched her up a little nose.

I laid the figure down upon the mantel, then began working on the next one. I gave him a blacksmith's apron and sturdy boots and a bald spot on the top of his head. After that I made Will, with his broad shoulders and long legs and fine, straight hair. I made a little hat for him, like the one he used to wear when he worked in the garden. And last of all, I made Margaret. She would be taller now—children grow like weeds at her age. But the only Margaret I remembered was the one who had run along beside me, throwing kisses, on the day I left the village. And so that was how I made her: a sweet, round-faced angel with plaited hair and a little winter cap.

Then I kneaded the remains of the dough and began work on one more figure—a boy dressed in a fine tunic with a sword at his belt. I wondered if I ought to put a crown upon his head, as he was a prince. But as I had never seen him wear one, I decided against it. I gave him boots and a long mantle, and when I was finished, I felt quite proud of my work. I had improved with practice, and Julian was the best of the lot.

As I held the little figure in my hand, my mind was suddenly flooded with memories. It was like looking down at my childhood from a high place. There we were, Julian and me: picking blackberries, sending leaf boats sailing down the river, playing tug rope out upon the common, visiting the fairy castle, telling stories, running races, sharing confidences, laughing about homely princesses, and admiring his beautiful falcon. Oh, how happy we were!

But then I came to that last day, at the fair: Julian in his scarlet tunic, sitting upon the paddock fence with all those handsome boys. And I saw him grinning and laughing—how could I ever forget?—then suddenly noticing me, and hiding his face with his hand, in hopes I would not recognize him. And I watched as he nodded to me so coldly—as though I were little more than a stranger, some upstart peasant whose attentions were unwanted—and turned away to laugh about me with his friends! I closed my fist over the figure, then, and Julian was gone, nothing but a formless lump of dough.

"Are you all right, lass?" Cook asked, for hurt and anger showed plain upon my face. I was not sure of my voice, and so I nodded and tried to smile.

Then Cook saw the figures, all lined up on the mantle. "Why, Isabel!" she said. "Will you look at that! Aren't they just like *real* little people! A man and a lady and a boy and a girl. It's a *family*, isn't it, child? *Your* family!"

"Yes!" I answered. And of a sudden the loss and the loneliness washed over me so that I could not help but weep — big, gulping sobs. Cook wrapped her arms around me then, and I leaned against her soft and ample bosom and breathed in the comfortable odors of herbs and onion and fresh-ironed linen. She stood there, holding me and stroking me and whispering sweet endearments, until I was done crying. Then she dried my tears with her apron.

"We'll set them all in the oven to dry tonight, just like I told you. And tomorrow I'll bring a little box for you to put them in. That way you can keep them safe — all the people you love."

What a rare good soul Cook was! I kissed her and thanked her and told her she was an angel. She just said, "Oh, pooh!" and turned away in embarrassment and went to take the pie out of the oven and get dinner ready to serve.

I would have to leave soon, I knew. It was time to join the others in the hall, where my clumsiness would be discussed and my manners criticized — unless I was lucky enough to be ignored.

Quickly, in the little time I had left, I set to work making Julian again — for I suddenly understood that it did not matter what he might think of me now. He was part of my past, part of my family. I would always love Julian, as he had once been. It brought me joy and comfort to remember those happy times. Why should I let bitterness drive them out of my heart?

That night—as every night since first I came to my father's house—I slipped away from the others as soon as the bell rang for Compline and returned to the kitchen to sleep. They all knew where I went. And they were glad of it, too, for neither Marianne nor Alice wished to share a bed with me. Though I now bathed as often as they did, my peasant upbringing would never wash off. As for me, I had no desire to sleep beside them, either, knowing how they despised me and shrank from my touch.

The kitchen at night was peaceful and warm. The welcoming glow of the covered fire gave off a gentle light, and the smells of the day's cooking still lingered in the air. I spread my makeshift pallet—a pile of old flour sacks—upon the floor beside the hearth. Then I went over to the oven and took out my little figures. They had dried hard, just as Cook had said they would, and felt sweetly warm in my hands.

I arranged them carefully upon the hearth, all the people I loved. They would stand there through the night, keeping watch over me. And as I lay in the near darkness, it was as though Will and Margaret were truly there beside me, breathing softly in their sleep, and Mother and Father were up in the loft, talking in quiet voices. And tomorrow, or the next day, Julian would come walking down the lane—and when he saw me, he would smile and call out "Princess Bella!" as he always did, and reach out his hand for mine.

And then peace passed over me like God's angel, and I slept.

# MATILDA

Sometimes I think God is having sport with me—like a naughty child who pulls the cat's tail. Oh, I know it is sinful to say such things, and I shall have to confess it to the priest. But it felt good to say it all the same.

Now I ask you—do I deserve this? Have I not suffered enough already, between widowhood and penury? Must we add a deranged daughter and a mad husband into the bargain? And then—and then—such a lovely surprise! "I have a daughter," he says. "You shall raise her," he says. "She has lived among peasants all her life," he says!

"Why not leave her where she is?" I suggest.

And what do you think he says to *that*? *"I wish to know if she looks like Catherine."* He says this to *me*! His *wife*! He might at least try to pretend he esteems me. He might hold off mentioning Catherine one day in the week, if only for variety! Not that I expected roses, or poetry—I am a sensible woman. I only want a little respect.

I believe sometimes I will lose my mind!

But I am ranting—and I know better, too, for it will change nothing and only cause my head to ache. I must think instead of my one consolation, my only source of pleasure and entertainment since I came to this unhappy house—my visits from Marianne.

Now that in itself is passing strange, for Marianne was never my favorite, being a willful child who was always complaining and insistent upon having her way. Never was she as sweet as Alice, or as considerate, or kind. But Alice is lost to me now, and I have only Marianne, who at least brings me amusing stories and gossip from court and opens a window into a happier world.

"Oh, Mother," she says, "wait till I tell you!"—and already I begin to smile. "Lady Ellen has been disgraced and sent away from court! The queen has had another tooth pulled, and you could hear her screams all the way out in the garden! The king fell asleep in chapel, and began to snore—and the priest knew not what to do, and so he feigned a fit of coughing, so as to wake the king politely—and when His Majesty came to himself with a snort, he glowered at the priest and said, 'Father, do you want a lozenge?'"

Marianne always tells good stories. Naturally Edward leaves the room as soon as she appears. He does not wish to be amused—it is *so* much more pleasant to mope about and be glum!

Usually her stories are of trifling matters, but not always. One day she had a most remarkable tale to tell. It disrupted our household, as you shall hear, and much else besides.

We were in the great hall, Edward being up in the solar and wishing not to be disturbed there. Alice was sitting upon a stool in a far corner, in the dark, studying her fingernails. Isabel was tending to the fire, one of those common domestic tasks she automatically took upon herself when the housemaid was not nearby.

Marianne could scarcely contain herself that day, such was the news she had to impart.

"The queen," she said breathlessly as she removed her mantle and sat down before the fire, "is *not speaking* to the king!"

"Indeed?" said I. "For what cause?"

"For the cause of breaking a vow—or intending to break it."

"You will drive me mad, Marianne. Do not be so coy. What vow is he planning to break?"

"The truce, Mother! The great treaty!"

I leaned forward with interest then. "Marianne — what are you saying?"

She was positively aglow. "Next month, on the fourteenth day of September, Princess Marguerite of Brutanna — the sister of King Harry Big Ears — is to marry Prince Adolph of Galant. It will be a very grand affair, as befits a royal wedding. All the nobility of Brutanna will be there, and the royal family of Moranmoor is invited also. There will be feasting and dancing and jongleurs and acrobats — "

"Marianne, make your point."

"Well . . . King Gilbert has *other* plans."

"*Other* plans?"

"Oh, yes — and they are the cause of the row up at the palace. You see, when it comes time to attend the wedding, the king will send word that he and Queen Alana are too ill to travel, but that his brother Julian, being already there, will represent the royal family of Moranmoor for the happy occasion."

"*Because?*"

"Because *secretly* he has raised an army, and *secretly* it is even now on its way to Brutanna — split into small units and traveling the back roads, so as not to raise suspicion. The army will assemble in the great forest near King Harry's castle and hide there until—"

"Until the night of the wedding," I cried—for suddenly I could see it all—"when they will attack *during the marriage feast*!"

"Just so! At midnight, when Harry's men are the worse for drink and revelry. And even were they sober, they would have their guard down, for they will trust to the signed truce and the presence of the prince as hostage. It is a most shrewd and crafty bit of strategy—King Gilbert cannot possibly lose!"

"But the queen considers it dishonorable," I said.

"Indeed she does! Mortal sin! It is bad enough, she says, for Gilbert to violate the truce, but to have his own brother's blood upon his hands—"

Then Isabel screamed, "No! Oh, no!"

We stared at her speechlessly—it was so unlike her, for Isabel's even temper was one of her few admirable traits.

"Isabel," I said. "Do not shout like a fishwife. You shall deafen us."

"But that is so horrible!" she cried, taking no notice of my rebuke and continuing in the same ear-splitting tone. "After *so* long, with *so* many dead—and now that we finally have peace, to start the war up again! Why?"

She knelt beside Marianne and tried to grasp her hands, but Marianne pulled away. "Stop it!" she snapped. "Don't *touch* me, you little rodent!"

Isabel sat back upon her heels and buried her face in her hands. "And they will kill the prince!" she moaned.

"We have just *said* that, Isabel, and the queen is most dismayed over it."

"But will someone not go there and warn him?"

"*No*, you ninny!" Marianne snapped. "It is a *secret* plan! You cannot *warn* someone of a *secret* plan—because *then it won't be a secret!*"

"Oh, poor Julian!" Isabel cried. "Did he not *say* he would die in Brutanna before ever he was wed? Oh, terrible prophecy! And there is no need for it! None at all!"

Marianne looked hard at Isabel. "What's this, ash-face? Did you go about eavesdropping up at the castle, back in your peasant days? Listen in on the prince's private conversations?"

"No, never! He said it to *me*."

"To *you*? I do not believe it."

"He was my friend, Marianne. My dearest friend!"

"Oh, amazing! Such lies you tell! Go away; I cannot bear the sight of you!"

"No, please—it is true. My foster mother was his old nurse, and he came to see us often. It is not so very strange—but oh, Marianne, it does not matter! His life is in great peril, and if no one from the palace cares enough to warn him, then *I* shall go there *myself* and do it!"

"You?" I cried. "*You* want to go to Brutanna and speak with the prince? Oh, this is too much, Isabel!"

"Perhaps—but I shall do it all the same. I shall *walk* there if I must."

She got to her feet and made as if to leave, and so I took her arm firmly and pulled her close and looked hard into her eyes. "Now listen to me, you ungrateful little fool. You will *not* leave this house. You will *not* speak of this to anyone. Do you understand? Marianne was most unwise to speak of it at all, for it is the king's secret business—"

"But—Julian!"

"Isabel!" I shook her to get her attention. "If it becomes known that Marianne has been repeating palace gossip at home—and, God forbid, if it should spoil the king's war plans—it will forever ruin any chances my daughter might have of advancement, and she is sure to lose her place at court. Do you understand me, child? I will *not* have you running about the streets, crying this to the rooftops!"

"Oh, Stepmother," she wailed, "would you have the prince *die* to protect Marianne's place at court? That is horrible! And I, for one, do not care a fig about her advancement, and would be most happy to spoil the king's war plans, for they are evil!"

I was astonished, for never had Isabel shown such feeling or been so bold. There was no question she would ruin everything. And so I did what anyone would have done in my place: I slapped her hard, then took her to the storeroom and locked her in.

# ALICE

*B*ecause I did not speak, they seemed to think I was not listening. They said whatever they liked in my presence. They even talked about *me* sometimes, as though I were not there. But in truth, I heard most everything—it was just that I didn't care. I did not want to be a part of the world. I would curl myself up, sometimes, like a snail retreating into its shell. I would close my eyes, and in that dark, tight space I would imagine myself growing smaller and smaller until I would finally disappear. I felt compelled to do this— but afterward, I was always still there, and the sorrow was, too.

Sleep is also a kind of disappearing, and I

tried that as well, for days at a time. But terrible visions found me in my dreams. And so I sought what comfort I could in dark corners, where the walls enclosed me and I felt less afraid. I would just sit there and listen. I had not the energy to do much else.

I heard about the king and about the new war and about Prince Julian. It did not interest me much at first. But then Isabel shouted, and that was strange; she never raised her voice. She was meek and hid herself away as I did—only in the kitchen, not in corners.

She did not seem afraid of Mother, but went on in the same loud voice, saying she cared not a fig for Marianne's place at court, and that she would go to Brutanna herself to save the prince, if need be. When I heard her say that, I felt something stir in the place where all the pain was. I remembered our terrible journey to the King's City—the mud and the cold and the hunger, the exhaustion and the fear of strangers, the blistered feet and sleepless nights in filthy rooms. That had been *nothing* compared with what Isabel would undertake for her friend! And I found that I loved her for it, and that strange feeling inside me stirred again.

I got up and went into my bedchamber. No one noticed. Mother was screaming, and Marianne was wailing, and Isabel was, too. I went over to my chest, opened it, and reached down to the bottom, beneath my winter underclothes, to the secret place where I kept Father's ring.

I had not looked at it in a very long time, for I had seen terrible things in that emerald. But I thought that if Isabel could walk all the way to Brutanna to warn the prince of danger, then I could look upon my father's ruined face, out of love. I had the strongest feeling that he wanted me to do it.

I took it over by the window and sat upon the floor there, where I could capture the light. And I gazed into the depths of that magical emerald and went on looking as a shape began to form in its green depths. And then, suddenly, there he was! But—how wonderful!—he was no longer a terrible corpse lying ravaged beneath the sea, but the dear, familiar father I had known in life. Such a thrill ran through me then! I drew a deep breath and felt my mind begin to clear.

And it was then, for the first time, that I understood. Father was not gone, as a flame is extinguished by the wind; he was in heaven with Our Lord, in a life beyond life, where he did not suffer and was at peace. And from that good place he looked down on me and sent me his love. Suddenly a great wave of relief washed over me, and my body softened as it does before sleep. I had forgotten how happiness felt!

It was at that moment that Marianne came into the room.

"*Mother!*" she screamed. Her voice was *so* loud, I wanted it to stop. "Oh, Alice, you monster! Mother, come here! Come and look at this!"

She had seen the ring.

Mother came running into the room. "What*ever* is the matter, Marianne?"

"The ring!" she shrieked. "That emerald ring Father gave her. She has it! She had it all along! When we were so poor we had to walk all the way here, when we had not enough to eat—she kept an *emerald ring* and never told us. Oh, you horrid little beast!"

And she fell upon me and slapped me and tried to grab the ring. But I would not give it to her. Never, ever would I give it to her!

"Stop it!" Mother shouted. "Marianne, for God's sake, get up! We have no need of it now. And if that ring means so much more to Alice than the welfare of her mother and her sister, then she is welcome to it— though it disappoints me terribly, Alice! I had thought better of you. And I have put up with a lot, you know, with your everlasting silence! Oh, I am disgusted with the both of you!"

Then she turned around and walked out.

"Selfish!" Marianne hissed. Then she left, too. I suppose she went back to court. She did not return to our room that night to sleep. Nor did Mother come, nor anyone.

The house began to grow dark. I heard the Vespers bell, followed by a door being closed and bolted; Cook had gone home for the night. Then all was quiet, except for the occasional sound of Isabel crying out and pounding on the storeroom door.

I continued to sit on the floor, listening to the night sounds—the barking of dogs, the howling of the wind, the splash of someone emptying a chamber pot out a window, then the slow, lonely peal of the Compline bell calling the monks to prayer. I waited yet awhile longer, just to be sure they had gone to bed, Mother and her awful husband. Then, at last, I rose up from where I had been sitting all that time, my legs so stiff I could scarcely stand, and hobbled out into the hall.

The shutters throughout the house were closed, and I had no light for my candle. But I could still hear Isabel, and so I followed the sound in the darkness, feeling my way along the wall with my hand until I touched the handle of the storeroom door.

I stood for a moment, listening to my stepsister as she wept and sniffled and sighed, just inches away from me, on the other side of the door. I wanted her to know that I was there, that I would help her if I could. But how was I to do that?

*"Isabel?"* I said. The sound of my own voice startled

me—it was so weak and soft, a broken thing, nearly inaudible. I had forgotten you must draw breath, first, to make the sound come out.

"*Alice?*" Isabel said, clearly astonished. "Is that *you?*"

"Yes," I said, more firmly, now. "*Yes!*"

"Oh, Alice, you are speaking! I am so glad!"

I was glad, too, but could not think what to say about it. So I just rested my cheek against the door and smiled into the darkness.

"Alice," Isabel said after a while, "Alice, please— will you let me out?"

"I was trying to think how to do it," I said, my voice still thick and hoarse. I cleared my throat and tried again. "Mother keeps the keys. Would a hairpin work?"

"It might," she said. "It's worth a try."

"All right," I said, reaching up under my headdress and pulling out a pin. I did not know exactly what I was supposed to do with it, but I turned it about in the keyhole for some minutes, with no success.

"Perhaps I should try from the inside," Isabel said. "Will you slide it under the door?"

I crouched down and guided it under. I felt Isabel take hold of it from the other side—and as she did, her fingers brushed gently against mine.

No one had touched me in a very long time— except for Marianne, who had slapped me. I had not allowed anyone to come near. And so now it was strange and sweet, that comfort of skin on skin. But Isabel's touch was much more than that—it was like rubbing your hand across silk of a dry winter's day: it made a spark that ran up my arm and into my chest and made me feel warm inside. I sat back in wonder as she struggled with the lock from inside.

"Oh!" she said after a while. "I think I have it!" Then I heard a soft click, and the handle moved and the door swung open.

Isabel knelt down, then, and took me in her arms. I had not felt so loved and protected in a very long time. It was like the old days, when I was a little child, and I would sit on Father's lap. He would stroke my cheek, and kiss my hair, and sing me silly songs. I think it must be God's will that we should hold and touch and comfort one another like that. Why else would it feel so good?

"Dear, sweet Alice," Isabel whispered, "what a lovely voice you have! And isn't it wonderful? We are *both* free now!" And it was true. I *was* free, released at last from a prison of sorrow that had held me as surely as a lock upon the door. I was changed all over now, a bright new Alice!

"You have done me such a service," Isabel said. "And more than you can possibly know, for there is something important that I must do, and you have made it possible."

"I heard. You are going to Brutanna to save your friend."

"Yes, Alice, that is so. And all I need more is that you should bolt the door after I am gone."

I did not really want her to go. I wished she could stay with me always and be my true sister. But I understood what she must do, and so I said, "All right."

"They will not punish you for letting me out?" she asked.

"No," I said, smiling. "For they will never dream I could have done it. You shall have all the blame."

"Good," Isabel said. "Now can you wait for just a moment more? There are a few things I must fetch from the kitchen before I go."

She was gone only a little time; then I heard her creeping back along the hall. "I'm ready," she said. "Come."

We were at the door. Isabel unbolted it, then turned and kissed my forehead.

"How I wish I could take you with me, away from this place."

"I'll be all right," I said. "I have seen Father, and he is with God."

"I never doubted it. He must have been a wonderful man—I have felt the pain of all of you missing him. Still, Alice, I do not think he would have wanted you to grieve for him so."

"I know. He told me that tonight."

"I'm glad," she said, and squeezed my hand. "Be well, sweet Alice." And she was out the door.

"Wait!" I whispered. "Take this."

Isabel came back. "What is it?"

"A ring," I said. "My father gave it to me so that I might see him in the emerald when he was away."

"*Emerald!* Oh, no, Alice, you must not give me such a precious thing!"

"But it is a magical ring. You can see things in it," I said. "Just hold it to the light. I saw my father there this very night. It might be of help to you."

"But if you can see your father in it, you must keep it as your greatest treasure!"

"No, Isabel," I said. "For it has already showed me all I need to know. I want *you* to have it."

I put it in her hand and closed the door quickly; then I barred it, and returned to my room. I slept easy that night and did not dream at all.

# BELLA

*I* met a tinker on the road, a kind-faced man with straw-colored hair. I suppose thieves and brigands may also have pleasant looks—still, I trusted him.

It was early morning. I had left the King's City but a short time before and was still unsure of my disguise, though Auntie swore she would never have known I was a girl, dressed as I was. My garments were those of her odd-jobs boy who slept in one of the out-buildings and cleaned the fireplaces and brought in wood and ran errands and such. We woke him in the dark of night to ask for his clothes. And though he was astonished by our strange request, he gave them up gladly in exchange for the money to buy new ones. To this outfit I added my old black cap to cover my hair, for I was loath to cut it.

Now I wondered whether my disguise would truly deceive a stranger, and so I plucked up my courage and approached the tinker. He had all manner of tools and implements hanging from his saddle, and they clanked and rattled as he rode along. The racket troubled Auntie's little mare; she did not like to come too near such a loud and puzzling creature, and executed a dainty sideways dance of avoidance. But I stroked her neck and assured her all was well, and so she complied, though she shot the tinker's horse a terrified look from time to time.

"Can you tell me the way to Brutanna?" I asked. He nodded; he traveled the north roads often, stopping at villages along the way to ply his trade, mending whatever pots and cauldrons and suchlike vessels as needed repair.

"What business have you in Brutanna, lad?"

I made a creditable boy, then! This greatly eased my mind, for Auntie had said it would be most dangerous for me to cross the country dressed as a girl — "And you almost full grown," she said. "Why, you're practically a woman now!"

This was true. I was no longer the gawky little twig of a girl I had been when last she saw me. More than three years had passed since the momentous afternoon that had marked the end of one life and the beginning of another. I had not understood, then, what a great change it would be for me. All I could think of was meeting my father for the first time, and what he would say to me, and how it would feel to live there and be a lady. I was all atremble with excitement and fear over it, knowing neither what to expect nor how to behave.

And then we arrived at that great, cold house, and I was greeted with such curt formality and unwelcoming stares that you would think they had been expecting a princess and gotten a toad instead. Only moments later Auntie left; she had not been invited in, and it was plain that they wished her to go. As she was saying her farewells, she became so tearful and overwrought, I half wondered if she had some secret knowledge of impending tragedy. It was most unsettling.

Her manner seemed all out of proportion to the occasion. Father was disgusted by it and told her sharply to stop making such a scene. Even *I* was perplexed. I did not like to say good-bye to her, of course; we had grown very fond of each other on our journey together. But I thought we were only parting for a day or two. After all, we lived in the same city now; she could visit me anytime she liked. And so I could not fathom why she wept so.

I understood it later, of course. Auntie was already well acquainted with my father's character—though she *had* counted upon his new wife to provide a gentle presence in the house. But a few minutes in my stepmother's company robbed Auntie of even that small hope. She saw clearly, then, what lay ahead for me, and it broke her heart. Moreover, she knew that, whatever I must face, I would have to face it alone, for she would not be allowed to come there to visit me, to give me comfort and ease my way. We were parting for a long time, perhaps forever—and that was why she was so sad.

It was also the reason she insisted, when first we entered the King's City, that we stop first at her house, before going on to Father's. I remember wishing we could do it some other time, as we had already ridden a long way, and I was tired and anxious to get where we were going. But Auntie wanted me to spend a little time with my old grandfather.

He had for many years been troubled in his mind—from old age and grief, Auntie said. All the same, he seemed delighted to learn that he had a granddaughter. He beamed with pleasure when I kissed his hand, and said how pretty I was, so like my mother. But then, after a while, he began to grow agitated and confused, calling me Catherine and scolding me crossly for staying away so long.

Auntie thought perhaps we ought to go. She tucked in Grandfather's blankets, which were in disarray, and kissed him on the forehead, and told him — as though he were a beloved child — that he must be very good while she was gone, that she would be back soon, and that Maddy the housemaid would be there at his side if he needed anything. Then we left.

Later, looking back on that little visit, I realized that Auntie had had another motive for arranging it, besides introducing me to Grandfather. She wanted me to see where she dwelt, so that if I should ever need her help, I would know where to go. And indeed, that is exactly what I did that night, after Alice rescued me from the storeroom: I went straight to Auntie's house.

Of course I *was* somewhat afraid she might try to stop me, that she would think my mission too reckless and dangerous for a young girl to undertake. At the very least I expected she would want to go with me. But she did neither of those things. She said straight out that she was not strong enough for such a journey, that she would only be a hindrance to me. Besides, she said, Grandfather was not well, and she could not leave him. But she was convinced that my quest was a righteous one, worth even the risk to my life, and so she promised to do whatever she could to help me.

We had had precious little time to work out a plan and gather the things I would need, for it was already late when I arrived, and I would have to be away by first light, before Stepmother awoke and discovered I was gone. And as there had been so much to do, I had not slept at all that night, not even for an hour. Now exhaustion was beginning to tell on me. But I was well prepared as to what I ought to say to any folk I might meet upon the road. And so, tired though I was, I answered the tinker easily.

"I am a messenger, sent by my mistress to her sister," I said.

"Have you papers to that effect? For if not, lad, you may be thought to have run from your master, and be taken into custody."

"I have papers," I said. (And I did, too, for Auntie had thought of that and had written some out for me.)

"That is good," he answered. "You will need them when you cross the border as well. It is not often that folk in Moranmoor send messages to Brutanna—truce or no truce. It is odd and might be thought sus-picious."

"I am sent to summon her sister home," I said, "for their mother is dying."

"I see. And the sister dwells in Brutanna?"

"Oh, no," I said. "She is with the queen's house-hold and lives at the palace. But she has gone to

Brutanna to prepare the way for the king and queen, who will soon visit there."

"Is that so? For what occasion?"

"A royal wedding."

"Ah," he said, and seemed satisfied. Then after a while, "Have you a good memory, lad?"

"Good enough," I said.

"Then I will tell you the roads you must follow, and where to stay the night that they will not cheat you—for I know the region well. Once you cross the border, though, I can be of no help to you, for I have never been there and have only heard ill of the people, that they are coarse and stupid and live like pigs."

"I have heard that, too," I said. "That they dine on fish guts and such."

He laughed. "Like enough they do," he said.

His good guidance saved me time and money, and may well have prevented some mishap that would have delayed me further. Auntie would probably say that God sent that tinker to speed my way—and perhaps she would be right, for I did believe my mission to be a holy one. I hoped at least to save a life, perhaps to stop a war. God could not but smile upon that.

In good time I arrived at the wide river that divides our two countries. To get to the other side I would have to take a ferry, there being no bridge or shallow crossing in that place. The ferry was little more than a raft of logs hauled back and forth by a system of stout ropes fastened to trees on either side. I boarded it with great reluctance; only pride prevented me from crying out when I felt the surface beneath my feet begin to move. My horse was likewise most agitated, and stomped about and snorted and rolled her eyes. I did my best to hold her still and calm her, lest she should cause us to tip over.

The boatman was surly and odd, with such a great tangled beard that it would have made a fine nest for a family of mice. He had one eye that looked at you and another that looked elsewhere. Indeed, I liked him not, for he put me in mind of Charon, from the old story—the one who ferried dead souls across the River Styx. Once this image had entered my thoughts, it would not leave me, and I began to wonder if the far shore would be like the country of the damned and its inhabitants the walking dead.

Dreadful as that prospect was, the river frightened me still more—so wide and deep it was, with such a mighty current. As we slowly made our way across, the boatman heaving and grunting as he worked the ropes, the force of the water pressed relentlessly against the rim of the raft, as if it wished to break us loose from our tether and send us hurtling down the stream. No wonder I was plagued by grim imaginings—I could not help it!

As if in a waking dream, I saw our crude little vessel capsize; I saw the boatman save himself by clinging fast to one of the ropes; I saw my horse, pumping her legs frantically in an effort to stay afloat, whinnying in terror as she was swept away by the power of the water; and I saw myself, too, swallowed up by the river, sinking deeper and deeper into the darkness, struggling to breathe, and finally dying there—my cap floating off and my hair fanning out around my cold, white face.

I have always had too much imagination for my own good. We did not tip over. I did not drown. We reached the other side with no mishap or calamity whatsoever. And once I had paid the boatman, I continued my journey north on a perfectly ordinary road. In truth I was almost disappointed, for the countryside of Brutanna looked exactly the same as that of Moranmoor. And the people I met there did not have horns or tails; they were not demons or damned souls—just ordinary folk, like those at home. Some were helpful and pleasant; others were not.

They spoke a dialect much like ours, though I began to notice, as I rode deeper into the country, that they had different words for many common things— *eggys* instead of *eggs*, and suchlike. Also, their accent was not so smooth and beautiful as ours, but hard and guttural. As part of my plan required me to pass for a local, I began to practice their way of speaking as I rode along. And I must have been successful at it, for the folk I met upon the road believed me when I said I came from the southern regions of their country. This eased my mind considerably.

I was stopped only once, shortly after I entered the territory of Brutanna, when I was asked to show my papers and was questioned closely. One of the soldiers looked at me hard, and I feared he had seen through my disguise and would arrest me as a spy. But my papers satisfied him, and as the upcoming wedding was common knowledge, and as the royal family of my country had been invited, they let me pass.

Everything seemed to be going well, yet I still worried about the time. I knew not how many more days I would have to travel before I reached the castle — and I *must* arrive in time for the wedding, if possible a few days before. And so I took to setting out earlier each morning and staying upon the road later before stopping for the night. Once or twice I was obliged to sleep out in the open, for I had already passed the last inn for many miles but had decided not to stop, as the sun was yet in the sky. I slept not well on those nights, for fear of robbers or wild beasts, but I came to no harm.

I have never ridden much in my life, excepting the

trip with Auntie from my village to the King's City. After so many days in the saddle, I suffered terrible pains in my legs and in the place where you sit, so that at times I could bear it no longer and had to get down and walk. But as this slowed my progress, I did not do it often.

Finally, at about mid-morning on a warm September day, I saw ahead in the misty distance the high walls and towers of King Harry's castle. I had been upon the road for a little more than a fortnight and, as I would soon discover, my haste had served me well. Three days still remained before the wedding.

# BELLA

$K$ing Harry's fields sprawled out across a goodly plain, a bright patchwork of green and gold. Brutanna had prospered much in the time of peace! The villagers, now free from fear of raiding parties, had built terraces up the slopes of the hills to the west and planted new orchards and vineyards there. And King Harry, no longer in need of defensive walls in peacetime, had begun transforming his sturdy castle into a grand and elegant palace.

They trusted us to keep our word and honor the treaty. They did not dream that in just three days, as the matins bell pealed the midnight hour, King Gilbert would ride out of the forest and lay waste to all that prosperity! Crops so patiently tended throughout the spring and summer would be burned to the ground in a night; tender vines and saplings, planted with such hope for future harvests, would be torched before ever they could grow a cluster of grapes or a fine, ripe peach. And Harry's handsome new palace would lie in ruins.

All this would come to pass if I failed at my mission. It was a great undertaking for a simple soul like me, and the weight of it hung heavy upon my heart. But I believed that God was beside me in all that I did, and that gave me courage. I determined to keep my wits about me and make haste, for there was little time.

I turned my horse away from the road, in the direction of the woods. We wound our way through the trees and tall brush until, at last, I came upon a small clearing not far from the forest's edge. Stopping there, I got down from my horse and began removing my boy's garments, folding them carefully and tucking them away in the satchel that was fastened to my saddle. Then I put on the old olive-green gown and round-toed shoes I had worn every day for the past three years. I would be posing now as an ordinary peasant girl—a part I could play easily, for I had been raised up to it.

I found stable room for my horse in the village; by

noon I had been admitted to the castle grounds and had found my way to one of the temporary outdoor kitchens that had been set up in the courtyard. This was common practice whenever noble folk gathered for a royal wedding. The castle cooks could not handle the multitude of lavish dishes expected on such an occasion—and for so many guests—so extra kitchens had to be built and help brought in to staff them.

I was hired on at the princely sum of one penny per day, plus meals. I would work under the direction of that kitchen's supervising cook, a broad-beamed, red-faced woman with a fine set of lungs. You could hear her bellowing orders over the din of the place like a pig in a slaughterhouse. She had a sharp tongue, too, and at first I thought she did not like me. I realized soon after that it was in no way personal. She didn't like anybody.

I had told her, when first I arrived, that I was an experienced cook—imagining she might allow me to make pastry or carve dragons out of marzipan. "Good," she said. "Let us see how experienced you are at plucking chickens."

But I could not please her, even at that common task. Pulling the bird out of my hands, she demonstrated by ripping out great handfuls of feathers at a frenzied pace, causing a blizzard to fly about our heads. "Like *that*!" she shouted, and thrust the carcass back into my lap. "We don't have all day. There's no place for lazy girls here."

"Yes, Cook," I said, and began attacking the bird with a vengeance.

"You must not mind her too much," whispered the girl beside me, a dark and robust lass with pink cheeks and a gentle voice. (She smiled often, and broadly, too—all uncaring that she showed the world a mouthful of yellow, crooked teeth. I thought this very sweet, and liked her better for it.) "There really is a lot to do," she assured me, "preparing food for so many—and such a grand feast, too, with all the royalty here!"

"Not *all*," said another girl, this one small and delicate with fine, yellow hair and a vexing cough. She did not trouble to turn her head away, I noticed, but coughed right into the food. I wondered that the cook did not rebuke her over it. "The king and queen of Moranmoor are still not here, and they are shockingly late! The other great folk arrived days ago." She counted on her fingers: "The king and queen of Galant (and the prince, of course), and the earl of Swithin, and the duke of Gran, and—"

"Oh," said I, "have you not heard? The king and queen cannot come! But Prince Julian is to stand in for his brother, and Queen Alana is sending one of her ladies-in-waiting in her stead."

"For what cause do they stay away?" asked the dark girl.

"The king was injured while riding," I said. "That's what they say. And the queen is confined to her bed with a complaint of the chest."

"A complaint of the *liver*, more like, from an excess of eating!" said the cook, who had magically appeared at my side. For such a big woman, she had a right delicate tread—you never heard her coming.

"From excess of *eating*?" I cried.

"Do you not *know* about Moranmoor, child?" said the cook importantly. "Why, even the *peasants* there are such gluttons that they break their fasts with duck in fig sauce, and wash it all down with a full jug of wine. Only *imagine* how much the queen eats!"

I opened my mouth to say that I had never in all my life so much as *tasted* duck in fig sauce—but then thought better of it. "Disgusting!" I said. "I prefer fish guts, myself."

The cook stared at me. Fearing I had said the wrong thing, I started plucking again, as fast as I could, telling myself very sternly to keep still and speak no more. Alas, I could not manage it, for such a slander against Queen Alana could not go unchallenged.

"I have heard it said that the queen is a very pious

lady, and something of a scholar," I said. "But I have *never* heard it said that she was fat, or any kind of glutton."

"And how is it you know so much about the queen of Moranmoor, girl? That she is too ill to travel and the rest?"

"Oh," I said, my thoughts racing. "I was nearby the gate at the time the messenger came from Moranmoor. I overheard what he said—that the royal family could not come."

"Did the messenger say the queen was scholarly and pious?"

"No. That I heard before. From a tinker who travels much about the country and gathers gossip from villages along the border."

"Humph," she said. "A tinker, indeed! I will have the queen *fat* and I will have her *ugly* besides. And you, girl, would do well to stop eavesdropping on messengers and repeating gossip. We have work to do."

I took this rebuke to heart and was more careful thereafter in what I said. All the same, I was well pleased that it had been so easy to plant my story about the expected arrival of the queen's lady-in-waiting. I made a point of mentioning her several more times, to a number of different people. There was already much talk about King Gilbert's absence, and each new piece of gossip was pounced upon eagerly and repeated at the soonest opportunity. No one would remember that the story had come first from me. By nightfall my tale would have made the rounds of all in the castle. This I hoped with all my heart, for upon the day of the wedding, in accordance with my plan, I would present myself once more at the castle gate—this time in the guise of the queen's lady. It was needful that they should be expecting me.

On my second day in the kitchen, I was put to turning one of the spits. Though this was not nearly so hard on the hands as plucking chickens and scouring pots, it was hot work, and tedious. I had to stand in the same spot for hours, slowly turning the handle of the spit so that the juices coursed down the sides of the roasting pig, basting the meat, instead of dripping into the fire and causing it to flare up. This was so monotonous that my attention began to wander out to the castle yard where the grand folk came and went, all decked out in their splendid clothes.

I watched them with special care, hoping to spot Julian among them. That would be an unexpected boon, for if I did not have to wait until the wedding feast to speak to him, then we would gain an extra day to plan our next move. But fortune was not with me; Julian was nowhere to be seen.

"Oh, look!" said the yellow-haired girl. She had

been chopping onions but stopped to point with her knife. "Over there—those tall fellows. Are they not the knights from Moranmoor?"

I felt my heart drop. "*What* knights?" I asked. "I did not think *anyone* had yet come from Moranmoor!"

"Oh, yes. They arrived last night. A very small embassy, though—only knights, and not *one* man of real consequence among them!"

"You'd think they would have sent an earl, at the very least," said the dark girl with the bad teeth, "if the king could not come himself. Do you think Gilbert *intends* to snub King Harry?"

But I did not respond to her question, for my mind was elsewhere. I was much alarmed by the unexpected appearance of these men from Moranmoor. Marianne had said nothing about an embassy of knights. What could it possibly mean? Dared I hope that King Gilbert had relented? But no—if that were the case, then he would have come himself, or sent the duke of Claren or some other important noble in his place.

"You will burn the meat, you careless girl!" said the cook, startling me so that I gasped and dropped my hot cloth. "Mind your work and keep your eyes to yourself!" she said. "Those fine gentlemen are not the *least* bit interested in the likes of you!"

"Oh, Cook," I gasped, my cheeks flushing hot, "I

never in the world thought they were!" But by then she had already turned away to scold somebody else. The dark girl made a comical little face at Cook, and the yellow-haired girl grinned and coughed into her onions.

I picked up the cloth, wrapped it around the handle once more, and went back to turning the spit. I gazed dully at the roasting meat, feeling sick at heart—for the arrival of those knights complicated matters greatly for me. They were sure to know I was not one of the queen's ladies; they had never once seen me at court!

"Are you ill?" asked the dark girl. "Shall I take your place at the spit? I would not have you fainting and falling into the fire!"

"No, no," I said, feigning a smile, "I am not light-headed. It is only a fit of indigestion."

"Ah," she said with a smile. "I understand. Cook gives me indigestion, too."

# BELLA

At about mid-morning on the third day, I excused myself to use the privy. I went, instead, to the well where I drew some water to wash my face and hands. Then I departed from the castle through the main gate. Collecting my horse in the village, I rode out once more to the little clearing in the woods. There, in the same forest where already the army of Moranmoor was gathering for the assault, I changed my identity for the last time. I took off my comfortable old peasant gown, folded it away, and brought out the finery that would transform me into a lady.

The gown was Auntie's, from an earlier time, before she began to grow stout. It was of ivory silk brocade, with flowers of a cream color worked into the pattern—a sweet and subtle effect. It was trimmed at the hem and neck with elaborate embroidery—quite wonderful it was, with birds and butterflies and flowers all intertwined with leafy vines. We altered the gown so that it would fit me better and be more in the style of the day—giving it a lower neckline that revealed the marigold *cotte* I wore underneath. The narrow sleeves buttoned from above the elbow down to the wrist—a task any *real* lady would have had a maid on hand to perform. I had to do it by myself, there in the forest.

I parted my hair down the center and braided each side into plaits high upon the head, which I then wound into coils and secured with hairpins. Then I carefully put on my headdress, which covered all of my hair. It was a padded construction of ivory satin, adorned with gold braid and seed pearls. It had little horns on either side of the head, over which I draped a sheer linen veil.

"When you wear such a fine thing upon your head," Auntie had told me, "it reminds you to stand straight and hold your chin up like a lady."

And indeed, I did feel like a lady when I first put on that headdress and that gown. But Auntie had not been satisfied. She said I must look grander still. I must wear jewels. I showed her Alice's ring, and she agreed it was extremely fine, but said I must have something more. And so she went to her coffer and took out a heavy gold necklace, set with emeralds. "There!" she crowed. "Wonderful! It looks well with the ring, and it sets off the gown to perfection—only, Isabel, I fear you must take off that ribbon. It looks most odd with the dress and the jewels, and it is soiled and threadbare besides."

"No, no!" I cried. "It is my talisman!" And indeed, I had not been without it since I was a child. It was a silver thimble that I had gotten from the fairies—well, in truth, I had gotten it from Julian in the *guise* of the fairies. I kept it in a little linen bag that hung around my neck on that selfsame soiled and threadbare ribbon.

"All right," said Auntie, "I understand. But if you *must* wear it, then we shall have to hide it." Once again she went to her jewel coffer and this time brought out a delicate gold chain to replace the ribbon. It was so long that the little bag tucked neatly into the bodice of the *cotte*, well out of sight. The heavy necklace and the little chain looked charming together, both of us agreed.

Then Auntie stood with her arms crossed and studied me for a while, squinting her eyes and tilting her head, so as to see me better—and declared me the *very picture* of a lady-in-waiting to the queen of Moranmoor.

"But, Auntie," I said, "I am barefoot!"

"I *know* that," she said. "I am still considering of the shoes." And indeed, she bit her thumb and twisted up her face in a parody of thoughtfulness. Finally, having reached a conclusion in the matter, she went over and unlocked a finely wrought chest that stood in one corner of the solar.

"I do not know if they will fit you," she said as she carefully removed some fine old embroideries and other fancy stuff from the chest, "but I believe they will. Ah, *here* they are!" She got up off her knees and turned to show me a pair of exquisite slippers—made entirely of glass!

"Auntie!" I gasped. "You are joking!"

"No, child, I am very much in earnest."

I took them from her. They were like nothing I had ever seen, for embedded in the amber-colored glass were tiny threads of gold, evenly spaced so as to make a pattern. In the front, two long strands met and formed a delicate bow.

"Did Grandfather make these?" I asked—for I knew he had earned his fortune in the glass trade.

"No, not Grandfather—a lad who worked in our shop. He was especially skilled—and most devoted to me, if you can imagine such a thing! He would follow me about like a puppy whenever I went to the work-shop. Indeed, he was the only boy who ever looked twice at me, Isabel, and so it pleased me more than it might otherwise have done. But do not think he was courting me, hoping to wed my father's money. No, he knew there was no chance of that. He just admired me, for whatever reason, with no hope of gain or advancement.

"One day Father sent me to have one of our goblets copied, for some of them had broken over the years and we would need more for Catherine's marriage feast. And there the lad was, blushing and proud, offering me these slippers! Oh, my stars! I think he fancied I would wear them to the wedding!"

"Did you, Auntie?"

"Goodness, child—have you not noticed my enormous feet? No, I could never fit into such dainty shoes. But I was flattered all the same—that he had seen me in that way, as a delicate girl with tiny feet. Methinks his eyesight was affected by the heat from the furnace!"

"Auntie, do not say that. I think you are *beautiful*!"

"Isabel, I was not fishing for compliments. I have long ago come to terms with my homeliness—and my large feet. I only wished you to understand that these slippers are more than just beautiful things; they were a gift of love from him to me—and now from me to you."

"What became of him, Auntie?"

"Oh, he died of the pox not long after. I took it much to heart, too, though I dared not speak of it, as people would think it foolish. I did keep the slippers, though—and there was a time when I took them out right often and thought of that boy and shed a tear or two over him. But that was long ago, Isabel. Let us see if they fit."

"Oh, Auntie," I said, "they will break!"

"He promised me they would not. He said he put the gold threads in to make them strong as well as beautiful, and added a bit of magic, too—he liked a little joke, you see. Come now, Isabel—put them on."

And so I did, though cautiously—gold threads and magic notwithstanding. Yet I knew, as soon as I slid my feet into those amazing slippers, that the lad had spoken the truth. They *were* strong enough to dance in (had I known how to dance, which I did not), and they fit so perfectly, they might have been made for me!

Now I stood alone amongst the trees, in my stocking feet, unwinding the linen wrapping from those incredible slippers of glass. I laid them carefully side by side upon the mat of leaves and pine needles that carpeted the forest floor.

All the while I had been dressing, I was preoccupied with thoughts of the task that lay ahead. It had made me increasingly troubled and anxious in my spirit, so that now I began to feel strangely unsteady and light-headed. It was warm in that sunny clearing, but I felt a chill and my skin was damp. I could feel my heart pounding within my chest and feared I would be sick to my stomach. And so I stumbled over to a rock and sat upon it, burying my face in my trembling hands. I had never felt like that before, never once in all my life. Still, I could guess the cause of it right enough: I was not ill, just paralyzed with fear.

It was almost comical. I had come so far and risked so much: I had crossed a dark, wide river when I knew not how to swim. I had ridden into Brutanna carrying false papers and might have been arrested for a spy. I had even slept out in the open, where wolves and thieves roamed the countryside. Yet now, at the crucial moment, when all I had to do was dress up and go to a wedding—I simply could not do it!

It had been easy to pose as a kitchen maid. I had not even minded playing a boy, once I was sure of my disguise. But to pass as a court lady—oh, *that* was hard. For all my stepmother's scolding, I still knew little of the customs and manners of great folk. *No one* was going to take me for a queen's lady-in-waiting! I could not dance, I ate like a peasant, and I doubted I could make even the most commonplace sort of conversation with King Harry's noble friends. Whatever did they talk about, anyway—their new jewels? Their troublesome servants? Oh, it was impossible! The minute I opened my mouth, I would fall into some terrible blunder and betray myself!

And even should I manage, by some miracle, to actually convince the other guests that I was a highborn lady who lived at court and was intimate with the queen, then I would be caught out by the knights from Moranmoor. For they were bound to hear that a lady-in-waiting had recently arrived from their country, and they would think it odd. They knew full well there had never been any plans to send one of the queen's women to the wedding. Naturally they would be suspicious. They would seek me out and know at first glance that I was an imposter.

But the most terrifying prospect of all was facing Julian, after the way he had treated me at the fair. And all I had done *then* was to wave at him and call his name! What would he think of me now, dressed so far above my station and in a place where I did not belong? Would he believe I had come chasing after him, all the way to Brutanna, too stupid to see that I was far below his notice? My face flushed at the thought of it. I could not bear to suffer his contempt a second time.

I spread my fingers and peered through them at the slippers, so dazzling in the sunlight—slippers made by a lad who had quietly loved where he had no business loving. Good for him, I thought. He had asked nothing of Auntie. He only wanted to watch her when she was nearby, and dream of her at night, and give her a miraculous gift. I don't know why that touched me so, and comforted me, and gave me courage — but it did.

I stood up and brushed the pine needles from the back of my gown. I had no choice but to ride up to King Harry's castle and face those haughty nobles, and those dangerous knights — and Julian, too, no matter how hurtful and humiliating the encounter might be. For if I did not, men would die that night in the thousands, and Julian with them. If I failed to save him, it must not be because I was afraid to try!

And so I carefully stepped into those remarkable slippers, and (oh, most miraculous!) felt a sudden surge of confidence. I grew bold, and sure, and strong! I felt as though I could walk upon *water* in those shoes! They would carry me safely through fire, protect me from arrows, or tempests, or fierce, wild beasts! Gold threads and magic, indeed! I was invincible!

And so, with a prayer of thanks to Auntie in my heart (and another for the poor lad who made my slippers and died so young), I mounted my horse — no longer astride now, for I had become a lady — and entered through the main gate of King Harry's castle one last time.

# BELLA

*I* had seen the great hall of a castle before;
we had slept at Castle Down many a time
when raiders from Brutanna came. But a *king's*
castle—with its soaring ceilings and blazing
torches, all decked out for a royal wedding
with rich tapestries and many-colored banners
and swags of greenery and flowers—that was
something altogether different! It was such a
beautiful sight, I gasped with amazement to
look upon it. And, oh, the gold dishes and goblets upon the tables and the musicians up in
the gallery making their music—I could scarce
believe it! I thought it must be what heaven is
like.

Nor was that all, for the king's guests were

every bit as splendid in their embroidered silks and fine brocades, set off with all manner of precious jewels. The ladies were visions of grace in their towering steeple caps and long silk veils. And the men were regular peacocks—such fringes and long sleeves, such scarlet and rose-colored linings and embroidered doublets and parti-colored hose and long, pointed slippers—oh, I never saw the like in all my days!

It dazzled me so that for a moment I forgot why I was there, and gaped and sighed—until I realized that I would do well not to appear so very awed by the spectacle, as I was meant to be a court lady and should thus seem accustomed to such displays.

I settled myself at the table farthest from the dais where the king and his honored guests were seated. It was considered the least desirable place in the room. People only went there if they could not find a better seat elsewhere. Not only was it drafty at that end of the hall—being near the door and away from the fire—but also it reflected poorly on one's social standing to sit so far from the king. It declared to all the world that you were a person of little consequence.

The nobility took such matters seriously; Julian had told me of it in the old days. I remember thinking how comical it was that anyone should care whether he was placed above the saltcellar or below, to the host's right hand or his left. But clearly it *did* matter; I could see it on the faces of my table companions — they were sullen and embarrassed. But I was right glad to be there; I *wanted* to be inconspicuous.

Of course, being so distant from the grand folk at the head table made it hard for me to see their faces clearly. I could not find any one of them who looked like Julian, though I knew he *had* to be there. Hostage or not, he was a prince, and protocol demanded that he be seated with the other royalty. I would just have to study the faces more carefully — slowly, and one at a time.

I began with King Harry, who sat at the center of the table (and his ears truly *were* big — I could see them even from the far side of the room). To his right was the bridegroom, Prince Adolph, and the bride, Princess Marguerite. And next to them were the prince's parents, the king and queen of Galant. The remaining two men on that side of the table were clearly not Julian, one being grossly fat and the other white of hair and beard. And so I began again with the king and studied the other side of the table.

The queen was to the king's left, and next to her, a broad-faced, fair-haired man arrayed in emerald green — the duke of Gran, perhaps? I moved on to the next face, and recognized, with a start, one of the knights from Moranmoor who had been pointed out to me in the castle yard. He must be the head of the embassy. Though not a man of high rank—or so the kitchen maid had claimed—King Harry had still placed him at the head table, out of courtesy.

And beside him was a slender young man, dark of hair and quite tall, with a crown upon his head and a trim little beard. He turned just then, so that I saw him in profile—and, oh, I was sure of it! Julian, without a doubt!

I watched him as he talked eagerly with the knight from Moranmoor. Julian seemed to be enjoying himself immensely. At one point he leaned away from the table and tilted his head back. He would have his hands on his knees and his eyes would be closed. I couldn't see this from where I sat, but I knew the gesture; I had seen it a hundred times. Indeed, I had provoked it often enough myself: he was having a hearty laugh.

It surprised me to see him so at ease; I had never imagined that Julian might be *happy* there, living as a hostage in Brutanna. I had pictured him going about the palace with armed guards at his side and sleeping in a room with bars upon the window. But seeing him there in his place of honor, dressed in such fine clothes and so clearly content, I understood that the life of a royal hostage was nothing of the sort. He was not a prisoner, not really. He was more like a guest, or a brother. Though Julian's new life had been none of his own choosing, he had clearly decided to make the best of it. Brutanna was his home now.

Well, I thought, now you have found him and are even in the same room with him—how will you gain his attention? In truth, I was at a complete loss. I certainly could not rise from my seat and walk over to the king's table and speak to him. It would be a shocking breach of etiquette—even *I* knew that. And it would call attention to Julian, and to me, when secrecy was most essential.

A fanfare of trumpets sounded from the gallery just then, and in came the pages holding high the dishes—all on silver platters, all fantastical in their presentation. The arrival of each dish was announced in a booming voice by a stout man with pink cheeks, dressed in royal livery (the head cook, perhaps, or maybe the steward): whole suckling pig! Lark pie! Wild boar in saffron sauce! Roasted peacock! (This one was quite evident to all of us, for it was garnished with a great fan of brilliant feathers.) There was a flaming plum pudding, a map of Brutanna made of fish jelly, and the wedding couple sculpted out of marzipan. Oh, it was beyond belief!

I thought of the fish guts and pigs' ears and other such rubbish that Brutannans were said to eat, and fell to musing about misunderstandings and prejudice and the nature of humankind. And then I became too busy eating to think of anything at all.

Once the banquet was well under way, the entertainment began, and it was every bit as remarkable as the food. No melancholy playing upon the lute here! No, there was an endless succession of fools and acrobats and dancers and fire-eaters and sword swallowers—indeed, every kind of clever and amusing performer you could possibly dream of.

But the one I liked the best was a dwarf who came lumbering, bearlike, into the hall, wearing a long gown, a comical mask, and false hair, his arms flopping like dead things. He danced about to the music for a while—then every so often he would turn quickly and lunge at one of the tables and make a little twitching motion—and *his mask would change*! Truly, I knew not how he managed such a miraculous transformation, but he did it many times, going from a white face to a red one and then blue and yellow and then back to white—and each one was painted to represent a different emotion, from a comical grin to a scowl and suchlike.

Then he came closer, and as I could see him better I realized that he was moving so strangely because he was dancing and walking upon his *hands*, and that the mask and hair were upon his feet and the flopping arms were false. And just as I was all in amazement at *this* spectacular deception, he slipped one foot out from behind the mask and began turning cartwheels! All in the hall gasped and broke into applause.

Finally he finished with a comical bow to the wedding couple and the king, who rewarded him with a purse of coins. The dwarf shook the little bag close by his ear to make the coins tinkle, cocked his head, made a wide grin—and got one more laugh.

Then a juggler came in (no doubt very bitter over having to follow such a masterful performance), and the dwarf, red-faced and panting, retired to the far end of the room, where he removed his mask and leaned against the wall to watch the rest of the show.

He was not far from where I sat, and so I motioned for him to come over, complimenting him and offering him a few coins of my own. Then, in a low voice, I asked if he would do me a service, for which I would pay him well. He said he would.

"Can you go over to the prince of Moranmoor, do you think? You know which one he is?"

"I do, lady," he said, "but I think the guards will not like me to approach too near the dais."

"There is something I would have you give to him, a token. I will pay you well if you will do this." He grinned at me in a knowing way. He clearly thought my intentions were less than respectable. "We are old friends from Moranmoor," I said. "I only wish him to know I am here."

"It matters not to me, lady," he said, still smirking, "but you must first tell me the price."

"Two silver ducats," I said, and his face showed that this was far more than he had expected—possibly more than the king had given him.

"You will pay? You will not say it now and forget it later?"

"I will pay," I said. Then I pulled the little bag from where it lay inside my *cotte,* and took out the thimble. "If you will deliver *this* to the prince." I put the thimble into his horny palm—in such a way that the others at my table could not see what it was, and would assume that it was money. Then he left to lean against the wall again, and I turned back and smiled at my tablemates.

"He was most extraordinary," I explained.

They acknowledged my remark with polite nods, then turned back to the fire-eater, who was just beginning his act. I glanced sideways to see if the dwarf had moved, but still he stood and watched. Then, with great subtlety, as though he only wanted a better view, he moved along the wall in the direction of the high table. This he did three or four times. At last he eased away from the wall and took a few steps toward Julian.

He did not get very far before a couple of guards stepped forward, grabbed him by the arms, and led him away from the head table. They cannot have believed that he intended any harm to the people sitting there; like as not, they thought he wanted to solicit money from them. Red-faced with chagrin, the dwarf returned to his spot, leaned once more against the wall, and waited.

After a while King Harry stood and toasted the happy couple. Then he announced that, although his gout prevented him from dancing, he would be most pleased if Marguerite and her new consort would lead the way. At this cue, the musicians in the gallery began to play, and the dancing began.

Now I watched with even greater care, so that I might follow Julian as he made his way gracefully around the room. He was a most accomplished dancer, I noticed (so far as I could tell), and received many smiles and nods from the ladies he partnered.

Once he passed close by me and I saw that he had not changed so very much—though he was much taller, now, and his chin was longer and his face more angular. And of course the beard greatly altered his appearance. Still, it was the same face, the same aquiline nose and dark curls and piercing eyes—except that there was *nothing* in it of the boy I had once played with! He was a man, now, poised and self-assured, a royal prince at ease with power and sure of his place in the world. And suddenly I was terrified again, for I did not know how I could approach this man, this new Julian. His village days would be nothing to him now, our past forgotten. He had moved on to greater things.

Just then, the dwarf saw his chance. He plunged in among the dancers and began imitating their movements and expressions in a most comical way, first as a mincing lady, then a somber gentleman, to the delight of all. Soon he had joined into the figures, causing great amusement when he ducked his head down low like the others, while going under the bridges, throwing kisses to the bride, and pretending to sport a shapely leg as some of the vainer gentlemen were wont to do. And then, in the midst of all this silliness, Julian swung by and the dwarf reached out and grasped his hand—and, God be praised, the thing was done!

# PRINCE JULIAN
# OF MORANMOOR

$\mathcal{W}$e had just begun the dancing when a clever little dwarf, who had performed remarkably earlier in the evening, came out upon the floor and joined us. He was very comical and entertaining, mocking us most unashamedly and making fun of himself as well. This added considerably to the merriment.

Then, as he was in the inner circle and I on the outer, we clasped hands in passing—and he astonished me by slipping something into my hand. I could tell it was a thimble, from the feel of it. And so, to free my hand for the dancing, I slipped it upon my small finger and took care not to lose it.

When at last the dance was over and all

were lining up for the next, I took the thimble off my finger and studied it. And how unexpected—how it set my heart racing! I knew that thimble well!

My mother had given it to me when I was just a little lad. I had been brought to the palace for my fourth or fifth birthday—I cannot remember which—and they had given me many fine and costly gifts in honor of the occasion. But the happiest moment of that day was when my mother had allowed me to sit upon her lap for a little while. I remember it still, how she held me close and kissed my hair, and said what a fine, big fellow I was. For that brief time at least, I truly believed that she loved me.

When it came time for me to leave her and return to Castle Down, I wept most piteously. So she sent me to fetch her sewing basket and took out her thimble and gave it to me. It was very beautiful, made of silver and engraved with the king's crest; I thought it the finest gift in all the world. Emotions are fleeting in little children. My tears were already forgotten before they had dried, and I left for my uncle's castle with a smile upon my face. For years I kept the thimble in my chest at Castle Down, and whenever I felt heartsick or lonely, I would take it out and relive the sweetness of that long-ago day.

And then—and then I filled it with ale and pretended it was a fairy flagon and gave it to Bella. Bella! She was *somewhere in that room*!

The next dance began and I stumbled about so badly and stepped upon peoples' toes so often—for I was scanning the crowd for her face and not attending to what I did—that Marguerite hissed, "Mind your feet, Julian; you will tread upon my gown!" And so I withdrew and stood aside—but still I could not see her.

Then I thought of the dwarf who had given me the thimble and looked to see where *he* might be. I spotted him at the far end of the room, talking to a lady in a cream-colored gown, who had turned away to speak with him. I saw her give him something—money, I supposed, for he smiled most beatifically and slipped the thing into his pocket.

Her business completed, the lady then turned around and looked directly at me—and I saw that it was Bella! Her fiery hair was covered with a fine headdress and she was arrayed as grandly as a court lady, but it was Bella, all right. I was so elated that I came near to running across the room and embracing her. But she made a small gesture with her head and eyes—"Outside," the gesture said. And so I nodded in return and walked as calmly as I could out into the hallway, most grateful that there was not a crowd there, waiting to use the privy.

I found I could not breathe properly. I began to feel giddy with fear and excitement and impatience. Why did she not come?

And then at last I saw her. She seemed to float

toward me like some heavenly being, her white gown almost shimmering in the gloom, her little slippers reflecting the torchlight as she walked—so stately and graceful she was! This was not the girl I remembered—the wild and impetuous child who was wont to run and tumble about and play games like a boy!

But then, as she passed by a torch on the wall and the light shone full upon her, I could see that she was only playing at the role of great lady, that her composure was false, and that deep emotion lay beneath the surface of that placid face. She faded into shadow again—and then she was there, standing before me.

"Princess Bella!" I cried. "Just look at you! All grown up and dressed like a lady, with jewels and a veil and such remarkable little slippers! And come all the way to Brutanna to send me secret tokens—what an incredible creature you are!"

She did not smile as I expected, but looked very solemn and almost fearful. "Is there somewhere we can go, so that we may speak in private?"

"We could go into the privy," I suggested with a grin.

"Julian, truly, I am in earnest," she said. "At any moment this dance will be over and people will come out here."

"All right," I said. "There is a storeroom at the far end of the hall." She turned and walked quickly in that direction; I followed after her.

The room was dark, so I left the door ajar, allowing some of the torchlight from the hall to penetrate the gloom. Then I took her hands and squeezed them in my excitement. "Bella, Bella," I said, "I am so amazed! Such a lady you look—truly, I would have taken you for a princess!"

"Not a princess, no," she said. "But I *am* a lady, as it turns out. The daughter of a knight from the King's City."

"More amazing still!" I said. "And you were enchanted by fairies and left in a cottage in the village of Castle Down!" I had not meant to mock her in saying this. I was giddy with joy and had merely fallen back into our old games. But Bella stiffened and drew her hands away.

"No, Julian," she said coldly, "I was *not* enchanted by fairies. I was taken to the village near my father's estate—Burning Wood, I am sure you know of it— and left there in the care of a wet nurse. Beatrice. The same as you."

"Indeed, I am right glad to hear it," I said lamely.

"Well, I was not," she answered. "For my father left me there all those years and thought not a whit about me until he married again. And I would far rather be as I was, and not a lady—for my father loves me not and treats me ill, and my stepmother likewise.

But I am wellborn, Julian, I assure you of that. You need not be ashamed to know me now."

It was a blow, and I deserved it. I ought to have apologized the first moment I saw her—instead of inviting her into the privy and mocking her with talk of fairies! What a thoughtless, clumsy, stupid, bumbling oaf I was! I would not have blamed her if she had wished me to the devil and returned to Moranmoor that very night! And so, while I yet had the chance, I fell to my knees and looked up into her astonished face.

"Bella," I said, "I left the fair that day and was upon the road to your house when the king's messengers intercepted me, bringing news of the truce and the part I was to play in it. I had meant to be waiting when you came home, so that I might kneel before you, as I do now, and beg your forgiveness. But, Bella, they would not grant me any delay and said I must leave that very hour."

She tried to interrupt me then, but I would say it all. "Dearest Bella, it had naught to do with your birth. Truly, you could have been begot by trolls, for all I cared! Only, I was so private in my knowing of you, and I was confused and awkward in the presence of those boys. And I was cowardly also, and vile—I know that. I did not deserve your trust or your friendship. But I beg you to look upon me now and see if I am not better, and try to like me again as you did once."

She leaned over then, as I knelt there—and *kissed* me! Now it was *my* turn to be astonished!

"You never lost my love," she said. "Nor could you. It was rooted too deep in my heart to tear out in a single day. Still, that was a very pretty speech, and I think it is well that you made it. Only now, dear Julian, you must get up off your knees and let me tell you why I have come, for it will not wait and is a very grave matter—indeed, your life hangs upon it."

"My *life*?"

"Yes, and much else besides. For your brother Gilbert is waiting even now with an army in yonder woods. It is for that reason he did not come to the wedding—for he will attack at midnight, when the men of Brutanna are tired from the revelry and the worse for drink. And if you are still here, Julian, your life will be forfeit."

I was so stunned I could not speak at first.

"How came you to learn of this?" I said at last, when I had found my tongue.

"My stepsister is one of the queen's handmaids. There was a great row over at the palace, for the queen was opposed to the plan and stopped speaking to the king on account of it. Naturally my stepsister heard it all and carried the tale home. But I should tell you, Julian, that she said nothing at all of an embassy of knights—and I know not what to make of them."

Oh, but I did.

"They are here to kill the guards and open the gate for Gilbert when he arrives. For Harry's defenses might be weaker now than once they were, but it would be no easy thing to scale these walls, and all advantage of surprise would be lost. No, my brother wants a slaughter, and an easy one. And do not look so stricken, Bella. Did you not know that war is cruel?"

"I know nearly as much about war as you do, Julian. Only, to come as a guest to a wedding, and sit at Harry's table, and eat his food—and then go out and murder his guards . . ."

"Is despicable," I said. "Yes. It makes me ill." I sat down upon a barrel and buried my face in my hands, for I was utterly wretched.

She touched my shoulder gently. "Julian," she said, "we have not the time to talk of this anymore—you must leave the castle, and quickly."

"Oh, Bella," I said, "I know not what to do. I cannot leave here in good conscience, for then I shall be conspiring in my brother's treachery. Father signed the truce upon his sworn oath, and King Harry has kept his side of the bargain and has treated me well. I would not betray his kindness thus. But nor can I warn him of the attack, for that would be treason against my own kingdom. Indeed, Bella, I believe I would rather hang for my brother's crime and save my soul than leave this place and live forever, dishonored and disgraced."

"That is very noble," she said, "but would it not be better to ride out to where your brother is and persuade him to turn back?"

"How could I sway him when the queen cannot?"

"The queen is a woman, and men such as Gilbert do not esteem us as they do men. They think us softhearted and foolish. But he might listen to *you*. It is worth a chance, do you not think? Can you not bend your pride *only a little*, in hopes of preventing a slaughter? For if this war begins anew—mark my words—we will never see peace again so long as we live. Oh, Julian, think how many will perish! It is too horrible! What good would it do to just stay here and die?"

"Well spoken, Bella," I said. "Pride was ever my weakness. It masters me and makes me addlebrained. I shall go to Gilbert, as you said—though I have not such high hopes as you that I can change his mind— for I know my brother, as you do not. Still, I will do all I can."

"Good! Only, Julian, I confess my plan only carried me this far. I do not know how we are to get out of the castle so late at night. I had hoped, as you know the place, that you might think of a way."

"I heard talk of a passage somewhere within the castle walls, built long ago for secret egress during sieges. But I know not where it is. We could spend weeks looking for it."

"Then it is of no use to us," she said, "for you must reach the king before midnight. We will have to leave through the gate, then. Perhaps I could hide you in a basket of dirty linen and carry you out that way."

"That is very amusing, Bella, but no one would carry laundry out so late at night."

She sighed. "I know. I was only being a *little* comical about the laundry basket, Julian. I was trying to think how to hide you. For even if we *could* think of a reason for departing at such an hour, they would never allow you to leave the castle."

"That's not true, Bella," I said. "These three years and more of peace have made Harry easy in his mind—far too easy, it seems. He would not expect me to escape any more than he would expect my brother to attack him this night. No, the guards wouldn't stop me. They have seen me come and go many a time—I ride out to hunt nearly once in every week."

"Well, that is good." We sat in silence then, searching our minds for some workable idea.

"Wait—I have thought of something!" Bella said.

"Tell me!"

"We shall say the king and queen of Moranmoor sent a message some days ago, saying they were now in better health and they *would* attend the wedding after all. But they set out late, and their journey was further delayed by a series of mishaps—a broken carriage wheel, or something of that nature—and so they missed the wedding and are only just arriving now. And therefore you and I—as prince of Moranmoor and lady-in-waiting to the queen—are riding out to welcome them and escort them to the castle!"

"That is very good, Bella—though the guards might think it strange for us to ride out alone, only the two of us, with no other dignitaries."

"*Or* they might believe King Harry means to snub your brother for his rudeness, by sending only you and me to greet him."

"How clever you are!" I said. "You always could tell a good story. That should do excellently well!"

"Then let us make haste," she said. "For it grows late."

As we stepped out into the hallway, I thought I saw someone moving in the shadows. I gasped and squeezed Bella's hand. We had been overheard.

"Halt!" I said. The figure stopped where it was.

"It is the dwarf," Bella whispered, then rushed over to where he stood, cowering in the darkness. She took firm hold of his arm and leaned down to speak to him.

"You!" she hissed. "Did I not reward you well enough for your service? Is this how you repay me — by spying upon me?"

"Indeed, no, my lady," he said. "I was only waiting for my turn in the garderobe."

"The privy is at the *other end of the hall*," I said. "Do not take us for fools. You were eavesdropping."

"If I heard a thing or two, my lord prince, I *assure* you I will repeat none of it . . . though I *am* a *poor* man, who was not blessed by nature and must live by his wits—and there are those who would pay me well to hear it."

"You are a proper villain," I said angrily. I hated giving in to his blackmail. Yet I knew—as he did— that we had no other choice, and very little time. And so I gave him a gold coin. "See that this buys your silence," I said.

He backed away from us slowly and bowed. "Indeed, my lord. It will be as you say. *Silent as the grave*." And then he was gone.

# BELLA

*I*t was Julian who spun our tale to the guards, and he did it right well, for he can tell a good story, too. He put in enough details to be believable, but did not say too much. And his natural authority made him all the more persuasive. The guards, asking no further questions, simply opened the gates and let us out. I could scarce believe our good fortune—it had been far too easy!

"Be awake and looking for our return," I called back, "so that you do not keep the king and his party waiting when we arrive at the gate!"

"We will be watching, my lady."

Julian gave me a sharp look. "Why did you say that?" he asked.

"Oh, Julian—it was only a small warning," I said. "It gave nothing away. If Gilbert is not to be persuaded, then perhaps the guards will be a bit more alert to movement out there in the darkness—or assassins sneaking up behind them. Would that I could warn the villagers, too."

"Never fear," Julian said bitterly. "Methinks the dwarf will do it for you."

"You do not trust him, then?"

"Of course not. Do you? He took my money—as he took yours—and now he will claim King Harry's reward as well. I only pray that it takes him a while to accomplish it. Can you not ride any faster?"

"No. It is not easy riding sidesaddle—I am not accustomed to it. And I cannot sit astride in this gown. You must go ahead and find your brother. I will wait for you over there, in the forest. See that clump of birches? There is a clearing, just beyond them. That is where I will be. When it is over, whatever happens, come and find me if you can. If not, I will make my way back to the King's City on my own."

"I don't like it," he said, "to leave you alone in the dark of night, at peril of your life from brigands or wild beasts."

"Oh, Julian! How do you think I got here? I have traveled these roads alone for many days and even slept out in the open once or twice. I am not helpless. Nor am I afraid. You have more important things to think of. Go now, Julian, and stop this butchery before it begins!"

"Bella," he said solemnly, "if I live through this night, I will come and find you — I promise. And when I do, I will give you a kiss to match the one you gave me — and never after will I have you from my side." Then he spurred his horse into a gallop and rode away, growing smaller and smaller until he faded into the darkness of the overcast night.

I knew I might never see him again. It is a perilous thing to approach a hidden army in the dark of night; the sentries might well kill him for a spy before ever he got to plead his case to the king. And even should Julian manage to reach his brother, Gilbert was not likely to be persuaded. What were Julian's chances then? Would he survive the attack — wearing only his party clothes, with no weapon but his sword and no shield or armor to protect him?

The more I thought of the dangers he faced and the hopelessness of his task, the more fearful and agitated I became. And so I got down from my horse, and fell to my knees, and begged the blessings of heaven upon Prince Julian and his holy enterprise — for *nothing* is impossible if God wills it to be so.

I do not know how long I knelt there in the road, but by the time I got up, my knees were aching so that I could hardly stand.

All was yet quiet in the night. I knew not the time,

but the matins bell had not yet tolled the midnight hour, the signal for the advance. Somewhere in the forest, great matters were being decided, but it was all up to Julian now. There was nothing more that I could do. And so I mounted my horse once more and rode to the clearing near the cluster of birches where I had told him I would wait.

I would use the time to make ready. For, whatever happened, it was likely I would depart that night for Moranmoor, and quite possibly in haste. It would be best, then, to assume once more my old disguise as a boy. I could ride more easily astride, and would be less conspicuous traveling across the country.

And so I removed my headdress and Auntie's beautiful necklace and gold chain and packed them carefully away in the saddlebag. Then I sat down upon a rock and began the laborious business of unfastening each little button on the sleeves of my lady gown. When at last I was free of my finery, I stepped—most reluctantly—out of those magical glass slippers. They had given me much hope and courage, and I might yet be in need of their comfort. Still, it would look right odd to wear them with a tunic and hose!

Dressed as a boy once more, I felt remarkably light and free. I could breathe again, and move with ease, after all those hours in the stiff bodice and tight sleeves of Auntie's elegant gown. And what a relief to take off my fine headdress and be rid of all those hairpins! I unplaited my hair and shook it out so that it lay loose upon my shoulders, the way I used to wear it as a child. Stepmother would not approve, but the gentle play of the wind in my curls was so pleasant that I was loath to cover them once again with my cap. Not just yet. Not till it was time to go.

I thought I heard something then, and so I sat there, absolutely still, and listened to the sounds of the night. But it was only the calling of an owl and the rustle of leaves in the soft breeze. All else was quiet. No bells, no hoofbeats or footfalls or creaking wagon wheels.

Of course, this meant nothing. Gilbert would not make his move till midnight. He might be marshaling his troops, even now, getting ready for the advance. Or perhaps he and Julian were still in conversation and all yet hung in the balance. Oh, how I longed to know what was happening out there in those silent woods! And how helpless and useless I felt, sitting on a rock, waiting and doing nothing, when so much was at stake!

I went over to my horse and I reached into the satchel again. This time I pulled out the wooden box that held my little dough figures, each of them swaddled like a babe in a narrow strip of sacking. I unwrapped them one by one and held them tenderly in my hands. Then I kissed them and arranged them with care upon the flat rim of the rock. They had kept me company through many a dark night, back at my father's house. Now they would stand watch with me on the darkest night of all—as I waited to learn would we have war or peace, would Julian live or die.

On impulse, I picked up the little prince once more and held him close to my heart, wishing him safe, and well, and triumphant. Then I returned him to my family and went back to putting my things away.

As I was folding the gown, I saw to my shame that the skirt was soiled with mud, from my kneeling in the road. Oh, poor Auntie! She had given me her most precious things, trusting me to take care of them. And now I had ruined her beautiful dress. I was frantically trying to brush the dirt away with my hands when I caught sight of the ring, Alice's emerald. I still wore it upon my finger. And suddenly I remembered—what was it she had said?—"You can see things in it? It could be of help to you?"

Maybe it would tell me something of Julian! And so, my heart racing, I dropped the gown and ran to the edge of the forest in hopes that the light would be better there. But the night was overcast, and even out in the open I could not see well. Then, of a sudden, the clouds parted and a shaft of pale moonlight shone full upon the emerald—a most encouraging sign, if you believed in such things!

I took the ring off my finger and angled it to the light. At first I could see nothing, but as I continued to stare, a blurred figure began to form within. The longer I looked, the clearer the image became until, with a sudden thrill of excitement, I saw that it was Julian!

I held my breath, so as to keep absolutely still. I feared to move the emerald in the slightest. Soon the vision was as vivid and plain as in life, but for the pale green haze that seemed to fill the air. I could see that Julian's head was lowered, as if in prayer—but his expression was one of terrible sadness. And also there was something odd about the way he sat his horse; he was bent forward and his hands were not holding the reins. And suddenly, with a sting of pain, I understood why: they were *tied behind his back*!

That was when I heard the bells—not the slow, steady peal of matins, but the raucous clang of alarm, familiar from childhood. Julian had been right—the dwarf *had* betrayed us! Moments later I saw torches moving upon the battlements and heard the shouts of villagers. They were rising up from their sleep, confused to hear the alarm at night, and in peacetime. I could see them in my mind, pulling on their clothes, wrapping their babies in blankets against the damp— and shouting, shouting.

I looked at the far edge of the forest, where Gilbert's army waited, and as I watched, a shadowy mass seemed to flow out of it, as if the trees were moving. The moon had retreated behind the clouds again, and it was dark once more — but I knew what it was I had seen. The army of Moranmoor was advancing. And *nothing* could stop it now!

How many would die before the sun rose on a new day, I could not bear to think. This night would mark the beginning of a new era of war, for none would ever trust a treaty again. And there was no *reason* for it; there was no righteous cause for sending good men to their deaths — only greed and arrogance and stupidity!

Terrible grief washed over me then — such aching despair and hopelessness and rage that I could no longer stand, but fell there upon the ground. It was as though I was wrapped in a cloud, and I could not breathe, and there was a roaring in my ears.

It is the last thing I remember from that night.

## SQUIRE GEOFFREY
## OF BRENNIMORE

*H*ow strange that Prince Julian should be in my thoughts at the very moment that he appeared—and so very unexpected, too!

The prince and I had been pages together at Castle Down, back when we were children, though we were never particular friends. He was always stiff and uneasy in our company. Perhaps it was because he was a prince and his pride would not allow him to associate too freely with the rest of us. He was often away from the castle, too—who knew where he went?

Still, we were together for nigh on seven years, and we talked often—as boys are wont to do—of that marvelous day when we would ride into battle for the first time, and how glorious it would be. I think we all longed to die heroic deaths—turning the tide of battle single-handedly, only to be overcome at the final hour by the force of a hundred knights! We would be famous! Bards would sing of our valorous deeds, and maidens would weep hot tears into their pillows over us at night! Such are the dreams of little boys.

Now our moment had come, and it was not glorious at all. We were about to attack our sworn ally—in breach of a treaty, by stealth, during a wedding feast. Worse still, we had sent assassins there, in the guise of wedding guests, to ease our way, so that we might slaughter our former friends without threat of peril to ourselves.

Oh, it sickened me. I think it sickened the duke, as well. But as we served the duke, and he served the king, we were all there, our little band. All but Julian, who would surely lose his life that night—not in battle, but at the end of a rope, if Harry had the time for it—as payment for his brother's treachery. And that is why I was thinking of him, you see.

And so it was very odd that he should suddenly appear just then. He was grandly arrayed, having come straight from the wedding feast, and sat astride his great warhorse, Bucephalus. But his hands were tied behind his back, and a sentry was leading him by the reins. Prince Julian a prisoner—what a strange vision *that* was!

"Is the duke here?" the sentry asked.

"He is not," I replied. "He is with the high command. But tell me, what have you done to the prince? Why have you bound his hands?"

"We could not be certain *who* he was—*anyone* might claim to be the prince. We thought it best to bring him to the duke and see if he would vouch for him."

"I can do so myself," I said, "for we served together at Castle Down for more than seven years."

"*Geoffrey?*" Julian said.

"Indeed," I answered with a smile. "Have you come to join us and win glory in your first battle?"

"No," he said. "I come to have urgent council with my brother." Then he turned and spoke to the guard: "As this good squire has assured you I am who I claim to be, and not a spy, I beg you to make haste and take me to the king."

"I must return to my post, my lord. Squire, will you take him?"

I said I would do so gladly, and made to untie his hands.

The sentry stopped me. "I think that is for the king to decide," he said. "For—pardon me, Your Highness—

but it is Gilbert we serve, and not you. There have been feuds and plots enough in royal families before now — and truly, it is irregular and strange that you should have left the castle at just this moment, and come to us here under cover of darkness. And suspicious, too, that you knew our secret plans. I cannot say whether you are in league with Harry and mean harm to your brother or no."

"Then leave the bonds," Julian said. "I do not care. Just take me to Gilbert, Geoffrey, and make haste."

We found the king far to the rear, waiting restlessly for the advance to begin. When he recognized his brother, Gilbert seemed most astonished and displeased.

"What's this, Julian?" he said. "You are meant to be in the castle, at the wedding feast! How is it you knew we were here? Have you betrayed us?"

"Of course not," Julian said. "Harry knows nothing of your plans. I only learned of them through a friend who wished to save my life — which *you* put in peril, brother, through this enterprise. But that is of no consequence. I came here to speak with you on a matter of the greatest urgency, and I beg you to give me fair audience, if only for our father's sake!"

"Then speak if you must," said the king, "but be brief. I have important things to do."

I only just managed not to smile at this, for it did

not appear the king had anything *whatsoever* to do—important or otherwise. The duke and other high nobles were in council even then, discussing strategy and preparing for the advance. But Gilbert was not among them—he had placed himself so far to the rear that I wondered would he even see the attack at all!

Julian nodded to his brother respectfully and began. "Some years ago," he said, "as of course you are well aware, our good father signed a truce with King Harry. He consented to all the conditions of the treaty upon his sworn oath, with God as his witness, and at risk to his immortal soul should he break his word. That truce did not bind two men only—but our two countries as well. Surely you must see this, Gilbert."

"Nonsense!" said the king impatiently. "Father signed it, not I. And if Harry is such a fool as to think I will abide by it—well, he shall soon regret his own stupidity."

"But *think*," Julian went on, "of those hundred years and more of fighting, and all who lost their lives in it. Have you forgotten how endless it was, and pointless, and destructive of life and treasure? Please, brother—reconsider! It is not too late, even now, to turn away!"

The king grew red in the face—and this I could see even in the dim light of the forest. "What—would you have me play the coward and run from a fight?"

"No, Gilbert. There is no fight to run from! You have not been attacked. There is only a truce you intend to break, and a shameful plot you have devised that will bring dishonor upon our kingdom—and upon your name."

"Dishonor upon my name? You fool! It shall be quite the opposite! After this night's victory, they shall call me 'Gilbert the Great' or 'Gilbert the Bold'! I shall be honored above all kings. How do you like 'Gilbert the Conqueror'? I believe that is my favorite."

I wondered, hearing him speak thus, if he knew that back in Moranmoor, the people already had a name for him: King Gilbert the Unfortunate. Then it came to me, with sudden horror, that he knew *right well* what they called him. He had brought his army here to *win himself a new name*! Men were about to die for the king's vanity!

"Oh, Gilbert," Julian cried, "if you *truly* wish to prove yourself courageous and bold, then abandon this dreadful assault and take your army home!"

"*Enough!*" the king cried. "I will listen to no more of this womanish whining! If you are *so* fond of peace, you have only to wait a few hours and you shall have plenty of it. We shall be inside the castle walls and victorious before the first lark has begun to sing. By sunrise there will be no Brutanna left for us to fight with. All this land shall be ours, Julian."

"With the aid of treachery and assassins!"

"You always were a weakling, Julian. It is well that I am king and you are not."

"Then be a *good* king, Gilbert, and show wisdom, and turn away from this butchery—for it is against all the laws of chivalry, and if you do this thing, you shall bring the wrath of God upon our heads!"

"The *wrath* of God?" The king laughed. "God is *with* us! Have you not seen how He has covered the moon with clouds so that our advance might be more stealthy?"

"Oh, Gilbert!" Julian cried. "Surely you cannot mean it—that the King of Peace would champion—"

"*Enough!* You tire me, brother. I will have you out of my sight this minute—though, in truth, I cannot think what to do with you. Perhaps we ought to tie you to a tree until the battle is over."

"Do not glorify your enterprise, Gilbert. It will be no battle; it will be a *slaughter*!"

The king turned his horse away, to signal that the conversation was at an end. Just then we heard alarm bells ringing from within the castle walls. Gilbert turned back, wild with anger, and hissed at his brother. "So *that* is why you came here, you traitor, to buy some time for your good friend Harry! You told him everything!"

"No, Gilbert, upon my honor I did not!"

"*Take him away*," the king howled, "for I will not look upon him any longer, lest I be tempted to end his life myself. Put him in the front lines, squire; *that's* what we shall do with him! Let him enjoy the view from there—for he has ruined all our plans!"

"Your Majesty," I said, "may I untie his hands, so that he might at least have the use of his sword?"

"No. Let him lead the charge as he is. We shall see what a nice *pincushion* he makes, with a hundred arrows in that fine doublet!" Then he spurred his horse and trotted off yet farther to the rear, making petulant growling noises in his rage. He put me in mind of a child whose mother had refused him a sweet before dinner. Heaven help us, I thought, with such a man as our king!

We rode back in silence. Julian, I supposed, must be brooding over what lay ahead for him—a dishonorable death, his reputation forever stained with the name of traitor. Or perhaps he was not thinking of himself at all, but only of the battle to come and how he had failed to stop it.

I confess it amazed me that he'd even tried. Not even the *duke*—brother to the old king, honored in war and admired for his wisdom and authority—not even *he* had dared to speak against Gilbert's plan. Who would have expected timid *Julian* to do it? A lesser man would have fled the castle and saved his own life instead of riding into the forest and risking all manner of danger to stop a massacre.

Suddenly I felt such a swell of affection for this noble prince I had disdained in my youth! I could not bear the thought of leaving him there in the front lines, bound and unprotected by shield or armor—though I *had* been ordered to do so by my liege lord, the king of Moranmoor.

"Shall I untie you, Julian?" I asked. "Will you fight with us?"

"I will not," he said, "for I believe this assault to be wicked and shameful. I refuse to be a part of it."

"Indeed, I agree with all my heart," I said. "Will you ride out to join King Harry, then? I will not stop you."

"I cannot do that, either."

"What, then," I asked. "Will you die like a dog?"

"No—like a pincushion!" he said with a bitter laugh. "But at least I shall go to God without this sin upon my head."

"You always *were* a strange bird, Julian," I said with a grin.

"True enough," he answered.

I turned away then, only to reverse myself seconds later. "To the devil with your everlasting pride!" I said, drawing out my dagger and cutting his bonds.

"Decide as you will what side you will fight upon! And may God go with you."

I left him, then, with the first line of knights, just behind the archers. Julian's sword would be of little use to him against a thousand arrows, I knew. But at least he would have his dignity; he would not die a captive.

And so I returned to my place among the duke's men. The army was already moving out from their concealment amongst the trees. The clouds had begun to break up by then, so that first the moon was glowing behind a cloud, and then it was bright for a moment, and then it was dark again. The king probably thought God was providing light for us to see by — now that a stealthy assault was no longer possible.

In the distance I could see villagers fleeing into the castle while the first contingent of Harry's knights was riding out. This surprised me. I had expected him to fight from the safety of his castle walls. He must not have provisions enough to withstand a siege, I thought. And his castle was more of a palace, now, than a fort. He had made the wise choice, then. Better to come out and fight us now, and not give us time to bring in reinforcements.

I felt strangely elated. It would be a battle after all — with danger on both sides. There would at least be *some* honor in that!

We rode forward in silence, with only the sound of

horses' hooves and the creaking of saddles and clanking of armor. But none spoke a word, and there was dread in the air. In the distance I saw the glint of moonlight on metal up ahead—the army of Brutanna, advancing upon us.

As soon as we came within range, our archers drew their great bows and sent a shower of arrows raining down upon Harry's army. At the same moment, *their* archers let fly in *our* direction. Men fell on either side of me. I took three arrows in my shield. And still we rode forward.

The time was drawing near when our two armies would merge into one writhing mass of murderous men, fighting hand to hand, swords slamming against armor, horses whinnying in terror, and beneath their feet the bodies of men, and parts of men, and blood everywhere.

Just then the clouds parted and a bright stream of moonlight lit the battlefield ahead. At the same moment, I heard the hollow thunder of a warhorse in full gallop. I turned to see from whence it came—and that is when I saw him: a solitary knight, riding between our two advancing armies, through a rain of arrows, carrying only a banner of purest white. He was clad in white armor, too—but in place of a helmet, he wore about his face a halo of heavenly flames, so that he shone like the sun! It was the prophecy fulfilled! The Worthy Knight, so longed for in the time of the Great War!

At the sight of him, the armies halted; arrows stopped flying. As the knight continued his ride— back and forth between the two armies, waving his banner of peace—a miraculous thing happened. The air was aglow with radiant light, the most beautiful thing I ever saw, and it was as if everyone there was holding his breath, such was the silence. Then all around me, knights and squires and archers and foot soldiers, all the men in the army, fell to their knees and laid their weapons down. Across the empty battlefield, the knights of Brutanna knelt also. Swords and lances lay everywhere upon the ground.

And then he was gone, the Worthy Knight. He disappeared into the darkness, and all was quiet for a very long time—until one by one, we got to our feet and began talking of it in hushed voices. Across the way we saw King Harry's men turning back toward the castle. We did not follow them.

Someone said that the king had ridden forward in a fury, to find out why the army had halted its advance. When he saw that the men had dismounted and were kneeling there upon the battlefield and laying down their arms, Gilbert was so astounded and angry that he rode about screaming at them like a madman, cursing and calling them cowards. But then he drew near enough to see the miraculous figure who still galloped between the two armies, all ablaze with light—and of a sudden the king grew silent and sat there upon his horse, transfixed with wonder. Moments later he began to cry out again, only not in anger, but in terrible pain. "I cannot see! I cannot see!" he cried. "Dear God, I am blinded!" And then he fell from his horse, insensible. The duke had taken over the command and had ordered a retreat.

I went looking for Julian, then, praying that he had not been slain in the first barrage of arrows. I found him still in the vanguard, and still upon his knees. Not a single arrow had pierced his fine doublet! Yet there were so many spent arrows lying scattered upon the ground, it seemed impossible that none of them had struck him! It had been a night for miracles, though—what was one more?

"Julian!" I called to him. "Was it not a marvel?" And I laughed at the wonder of it.

He got to his feet and embraced me long and hard. "It was a marvel indeed, Geoffrey," he said. "Though I fear you shall have to take up farming now—find yourself a comely wife and sire many children and sit by the fire and play sweet melodies upon the lute. For the world has changed this night, and has no more need for your sword."

# PRINCE JULIAN
# OF MORANMOOR

*Y*ou will think it ungrateful of me, that after such a miracle I could find it in my heart to be angry with God. For was not a war averted and peace restored? Did I not ride in the vanguard, with no shield or armor to protect me—and live? And is not my brother Gilbert now as tamed by his blindness as a hooded falcon—so that he turns to me for advice, and is moderate and mild, as he never was before?

These are wondrous works, and amazing, and good. But, still—could He not have saved Bella, too? Was such a small gift not within His power?

That night when, just at the decisive

moment, the Worthy Knight appeared upon the field of battle and rode through a hail of arrows, causing two mighty armies to stop their advance and lay down their arms and embrace the cause of peace—after all that had happened, I went to find Bella near the birches where she said she would wait. My heart was near to bursting with joy. I had not thought the world had that much goodness in it, and I could scarcely wait to tell her of it.

But when I reached the spot, she was not there. Her horse was gone, and upon the ground I found her dress—ripped apart and stained with mud. There, too, lay her amazing slippers, and a collection of little figures, standing guard most pitifully upon a rock. There was a black wool cap, such as peasants wear in wintertime. And some distance away, at the edge of the forest, I found Bella's emerald ring. Oh, such terrible evidence!

I returned to the army in haste, hoping to enlist some men to help me search for her. But by the time I got there, the troops were on the move, already heading south toward Moranmoor. I rode forward, looking for my uncle, and finally found him at the front, riding beside the cart that carried my brother. The king lay unconscious, though he did not appear to suffer any pain. Indeed, upon his face there was an expression of perfect peacefulness. I knew not whether God had struck him down as punishment for his sins, or whether He had chosen my brother, as He chose Saul so long ago on the road to Damascus, calling him to turn from his wickedness and do the Lord's work in the world. Whichever it was, I did not doubt that the hand of God was upon my brother that day.

When I approached my uncle, he was most astonished to see me. He had heard nothing of my arrival at the camp earlier in the evening or my quarrel with Gilbert. When I told him how it was I came to be with the army, and of all that Bella had undertaken for my sake, and for the cause of peace, the duke was greatly moved. He most willingly gave me a score of men to search the woods and fields for any sign of her.

We left right away, for I was near frantic to get back to that clearing—though in truth, I had little hope of finding her alive. But at least I could bring her home for a decent burial, with all the honors she deserved.

We combed the woods and the countryside nearby for three whole days, but we did not find her. And so I grew angry with God and said blasphemous things and wept hot tears at the injustice of it, and the terrible pity.

Then I returned to Moranmoor, to act as regent for my brother until he came to himself and could rule once more. We had a holy truce now and needed no hostage to guarantee that which God had decreed.

I dreamed of Bella some nights, as she was when we were children. And when I woke, I could not believe she was no longer on this earth, so vivid was my vision of her. And so, remembering that she had said she would make her own way back to Moranmoor if I did not come, I began to hope that she had just been traveling all that time. Perhaps she had seen the armies advancing upon one another and had been frightened by it, and had ridden away in haste, leaving her treasures behind.

Of course this did not explain the torn dress. Moreover, she had *said* she would wait for me, and that she was not afraid, and I believed her on both counts. All the same, I clung to this one little hope, for I had no other.

Thus I went to the queen and asked if she had in her household a girl whose mother had recently married a knight, a widower with one daughter.

"Marianne," she said. "She *was* in my household, but is no more."

"For what cause did you send her away?" I asked.

"For gossiping of private matters, and telling state secrets about the town."

"*That* is the very one I am seeking!" I said.

"The girl believed I would protect her, because I liked not Gilbert's plans. She came to me and said that she had endeavored to stop the war by sending her stepsister to *you*, Julian. Imagine! She thought I would embrace her for it."

"But you did not favor the attack—is that not so?"

"I did not. I thought it deeply wrong and shameful. But it was none of *her* affair. I will have no one in my household who cannot be trusted to keep her tongue."

"Will you tell me where she dwells, this girl? For I seek her stepsister, who was my dearest friend. She risked much to save me from a certain death."

The queen looked down at her hands then, embarrassed—for it had been Gilbert who had put my life in peril, and she knew this right well, and was ashamed of it. "Truly, Julian, I will do all I can to help you."

And so she told me, and I went there—to the house of Sir Edward and his wife, Matilda.

They were most astonished to see me. Matilda flushed scarlet when first I was announced by the housemaid, but she recovered herself with admirable speed and was soon offering me a seat by the fire and sending the maid to bring me wine.

Sir Edward was upstairs in the solar when I arrived, and had to be sent for. When he came into the hall, he bowed low and greeted me respectfully, as was proper. But after that, he said little, speaking only when questioned directly.

Besides Sir Edward and his wife—and the maid— I saw only Matilda's two daughters from her first marriage. The eldest—the infamous Marianne—was quite handsome, I thought, though she had a bold, flirtatious manner I did not like. And the younger one, Alice, seemed strangely withdrawn. Bella was nowhere to be seen. And so I decided to ask my questions quickly, then be gone—for I did not like these people much and cared not to prolong my visit to their house.

"You have another daughter?" I asked Sir Edward. "Isabel?"

He nodded. "Yes, my lord." Matilda and Marianne exchanged looks of astonishment. Bella must have spoken of me in their hearing, I thought, and they had not believed her—that she could possibly *know* a prince, much less be *friends* with one. They would be just the sort to mock her over it, too. It pleased me to watch their consternation now.

"When did you see her last?" I asked.

"More than a month ago," he said. "She left the house in the dead of night and we have not seen her since."

My heart sank. "And you have had no message from her?"

"No. Nothing at all."

I had with me Bella's things, wrapped in a sheep-skin. And so I laid the package down upon the floor and unfolded it carefully. It stung me each time I looked at them—most especially the torn gown with its implied tale of violent death.

"Do you recognize these?" I asked.

The women knelt around the sheepskin to look, exclaiming over the glass slippers and the fine brocade of the ruined dress.

"This is her old cap," Matilda said. "But we have never seen these other things before. The night she left she was still wearing her peasant . . . the clothes she came to us in. She had nothing so fine as this. I think they must belong to someone else."

"No," I said. "She was wearing them when last we were together, the night she disappeared."

"What are these?" Matilda asked, picking up one of the dough figures. I had brought only four of them. I had not been able to part with the last one, the skinny little princeling.

I looked Bella's stepmother hard in the eyes. "That is her family," I said.

She seemed puzzled, and put her hand to her heart as though to ask—*me*?

"No," I said. "Her *family*. Beatrice and Martin and Will and Margaret. The people who loved her and cared for her all those years."

At that, Sir Edward flushed and turned his head away—and I was very glad, too, for he *should* be ashamed!

"Your Highness?" It was Alice, the younger girl.

"Was there not a ring? An emerald ring?"

"Yes!" I cried, startled, and held out my hand to show her, for I wore it upon my little finger. Alice took hold of my hand to look at it, forgetting in her excitement that I was a prince and that to touch me so was a breach of propriety.

"It was *my* ring!" she said. "Father gave it to me — and I gave it to Isabel on the night she left." And then she let go of my hand and hung her head and began to weep. "She is dead, isn't she?"

"Yes," I answered. "I fear she is."

We all sat in silence for a while, gazing down at Isabel's ruined lady costume lying there before us, and the little dolls she had made, and the coarse wool cap—all that was left of her now. Then Alice looked up at me again, her eyes bright.

"Did you look into the stone?" she asked eagerly. "Perhaps she is there. You could see. It might tell you something."

"I do not understand you, child."

"Here, come over by the window and I will show you. Hold it thus—see how the light strikes it? Now look inside, and perhaps Isabel will be there. It is a magical ring. I saw my father in it many times, even after he died."

I looked at Alice for a moment—to judge if she was not right in her mind, or if she was only making sport of me—but I decided she was in earnest. And so I looked into the emerald as she directed. And strangely, I *did* see something there, though I could make no sense of it. The image was dark.

"Keep looking," she whispered. She was standing close to me, her hand upon my arm. "It takes a while. You will see it better in a moment."

And gradually it *did* become clearer. I was looking into a dark room, or perhaps it was the dark corner of a room. A poor cottage, it seemed, with a straw pallet, and a figure lying upon it.

"Can you see her?" Alice asked. "Is she there?"

"I *do* see something. Or some*one*. Only, Alice—it is not Isabel. It's a man."

"Oh," she said.

"But how strange this is!" I cried. And indeed, I could scarce believe it—but the more I looked, the more certain I became. "I had not thought him mortal," I said, more to myself than to her.

"Who?" This from Marianne, who had been hovering nearby, listening.

"The knight—he who saved us all. I thought he was some heavenly being, sent by God. Yet I see him lying wounded in a peasant cottage, like any man—though in the same white armor as before. And there is still the flame about his head. Only it is not so bright as it was."

"Let me see!" said Marianne, and she pushed in between Alice and me, and grabbed my hand with the ring on it. I lost the light, then, and the vision was gone.

"*Lady*, you are too *familiar*!" I snapped, and pulled my hand away. She cringed, as I had meant her to, and slunk away. Still, Alice stayed where she was, calmly watching me.

"It's all right," she said. "It will be there again, when next you look. Only—how I wish it had been Isabel you saw!"

"Alice," I said, "I know by rights this ring belongs to you. But I had thought to wear it always, in her memory. It comforts me mightily."

"Oh, no, my lord prince, it is yours now. I gave it to Isabel, and I believe she would have wanted you to have it. And besides, it has spoken to me already, and given me comfort. And I believe it guided Isabel when she was in need of it. Now it speaks to you. There is a reason you saw what you did when you looked into that stone."

"What do you mean, Alice—a reason?"

"The knight must be in need of you," she said. "Else you would not see him there."

"I cannot fathom it," I admitted. "I thought him an angel! He brought two armies to their knees! How could such a being now lie wounded in some hovel, like any common mortal?"

"Is that what you saw?"

"That is *exactly* what I saw."

"Then it is true. You should go and find him," she said. "And see what he wants."

"But I know not where he is!"

"The ring will guide you," she said. "I am sure of it."

"Then I will go. And if you are willing, I would have you come with me. For I think God has called you also to this task."

Her face beamed then—and suddenly she became a very different Alice from the shy, downcast girl of moments before. She was now a radiant young lady, confident and full of spirit.

"Oh, *yes*!" she cried.

# ALICE

*O*h, Father, I have such an amazing story to tell you—I think you will scarce believe it!

Remember how I longed to go adventuring with you when I was little? Well, now I have had an adventure of my own! Of course it was not quite so wonderful as it would have been to sail off with you to exotic lands and see the strange, wild creatures that dwell in those places, and meet all the pashas and the sultans. But I know that can never be, for you are in God's arms now. All the same, I am sure you hear me up there in heaven, and think of me often and love me as much as you did before you died. And so I know it will delight you to hear that I have traveled *all the way to Brutanna* with a *royal prince,* at his *personal request*!

See? I knew I would astonish you!

But wait—there is yet more! We went there to rescue the Worthy Knight! And we found him, too—and *such* a miraculous and confounding event *that* was! I am sure you know the knight of whom I speak—I think all in heaven must have peered over the clouds to watch and cheer his amazing ride. Well, we saw him in your emerald ring, Father, lying wounded in a humble cottage! It seemed wondrous strange to us, Prince Julian and me, that such a miraculous being could be truly mortal, at risk of harm like any common man. But I suppose that only one who loved peace enough to die for it had the power to bring about such a miracle.

How dreadful, then, that he should lie untended in a hovel—perhaps even upon the point of death—after all the good he had done! And so, on the very day we learned of his plight, we rode out to come to his aid.

The prince was accompanied by a great many nobles, as well as the king's physician, who would tend to the knight should we find him. And Father—you need not fear there was any impropriety, that I rode among all those men unchaperoned—for *Queen Alana came also,* together with the ladies of her household! She went to give thanks and to do penance, she said. Oh, Father, the queen is not haughty or proud, as you might expect her to be, but kind and good. She treated me with the greatest kindness and said she wished me to come to court and be one of her ladies. But I fear that would injure Marianne's feelings—for the queen sent *her* away. I guess you already heard about that.

We traveled at a brisk pace, so anxious was the prince to find the knight, and so afraid that he might die before ever we got there. We were guided all the way by your ring, and Prince Julian would have me beside him at all times so that I might interpret what he saw in it. There was no real need of this, though, for the visions came to him and not to me. He would see a mountain there in the emerald, or a winding road, or a copse of trees—and always we would come upon that very mountain or road or trees soon after, and know we were headed aright. Still, I was glad he wished for me to be at his side, for he is a most splendid prince, Father, and handsome and good.

As we rode north, there was much talk among the people as to where we were going and why. Many of them joined our procession—common folk and highborn alike—as though they went on a pilgrimage. This happened in Brutanna as well as in Moranmoor.

Our numbers had grown to several hundred, I would guess, by the time we left the main road and headed into the countryside, to the west of where King Harry's castle stands. The soil in those parts is rocky and poor, not fit for farming, and so it was used for the grazing of sheep. The way soon grew so narrow that no two could ride together, and it was so uneven that we were forced to slow our pace. If ever there was a spot where you would expect to find a humble cottage, this was it.

We came over a rise, and suddenly Prince Julian spurred his horse into a trot. I knew then that he had seen the place where the knight lay. And indeed, moments later I saw it, too—a little hut so small and ill favored that you would not even think to call it a cottage. Shelter from wind and rain was all it could provide—and precious little of that, as it had no door, and the walls were cracked, and the thatched roof had a great gaping hole in it.

Near the entrance stood a ragged child of about eight or nine years of age. He was wild-eyed with fear but seemed powerless to move from the spot, so transfixed was he by the sight of such a crowd of people, and the prince, and his knights, all so splendidly arrayed. Nor could he speak with enough force so that anyone could hear him. But he indicated with whispers and gestures that someone else—a father or a grandfather, perhaps—also lived there, but that he was away, most likely looking after the sheep. When asked if a wounded knight lay within, he merely pointed at the door. Finally, when the prince dismounted and made toward the entrance of the hut, the child found his feet *and* his voice, and fled wailing into the small copse of trees nearby, from whence he did not return.

Before Julian went inside, he turned and looked for me—I stood close behind him—and he took my hand and squeezed it. I felt his fear and hope and excitement all joined together in that touch. Then he let go of my hand and bent his head and ducked through the little opening, into the shadowy space within.

The only light in the room came from the door—now well blocked by those of us who peered through it—and from the smoke hole above. But the angle of the sun was such that a beam of light came through the roof and shone directly upon the figure that lay at Julian's feet. And I saw it then—the fiery nimbus I had heard spoken of, radiating from the head of the sleeping knight, like a magical helmet of flame. Julian knelt before the knight and spoke softly to him.

I watched intently, and in time my eyes adjusted to the dark so that I was better able to see. And Father— how I blinked in astonishment, hardly believing the evidence of my own eyes! And how I gaped in amazement, for I realized that all I had seen before had been an illusion! The knight's head was not framed by a halo of fire, but a tangle of reddish gold hair, lit bright by the sun. And he wore no armor—only a soiled tunic of a buff color, and torn hose.

Julian bent over and laid his head upon the pallet beside the figure. I saw his body shake, as from a convulsive sob, and I feared we had arrived too late. But then the knight turned his head and—I could not catch my breath, such was the shock of it. For, Father, it was not a knight at all, or even a man. It was *Isabel*!

She opened her eyes and touched Julian's hair. He lifted his head and gazed at her, unspeaking.

"Julian!" she said. "On your knees, *yet again*?"

"Oh, Bella!" he said, almost laughing, but for the tears.

"I fell off my horse. Was that not clumsy of me? I fear I broke my leg—and took a few arrows in my shoulder, too. But I'm better now." She looked toward the door, then, and saw me, and all the others crowding around the small entrance. "Is that *Alice*?" she asked drowsily, squinting in my direction. "There are such a lot of people, Julian!"

"Yes," he said.

"The battle must be over," she said, "or else you would not be here. What happened?"

"*You* happened, Bella. You saved us."

He kissed her, then, and I looked away, for it

seemed not right to stare. It was then that I saw, leaning against the wall of the hut, a stout branch with a torn strip of ivory brocade tied to one end. Of course! The banner of peace!

It had been a miracle after all: A young woman dressed in shabby boy's clothes had become a great knight in white armor. Golden hair became a wreath of flame. A branch and a fragment torn from a gown were transformed into a noble banner. Everyone saw what God wished him to see. Only the courage and the danger were real—and they had all been hers.

"Bella," Julian said. "Can you rise from your bed?"

"I have been considering it," she said, "though I do not think I can stand without aid."

And so he lifted her up in his arms and carried her out into the daylight. We all stepped back to make way for him—except one or two knights who helped him ease her through the narrow door. There was much gasping and whispering among the people when they saw her, for they had expected to see a strapping knight aglow with celestial light, not a girl of sixteen with dirt upon her face and bits of straw in her hair.

The prince helped her balance on her good leg for a moment. It was lovely to see them together thus: Julian so fine in his royal tunic, his crown upon his head, and his arm about my stepsister—who was bandaged and rumpled and beaming like the sun.

"Bella," he said softly. "Will you kneel? Can you do it?"

"More easily than I can stand," she said. "Is it *my* turn to make a pretty speech then, Julian? *I most sincerely regret that I did not wait for you, as promised?*"

"No, Bella, I only need you to kneel for a moment. Try to stay upright if you can."

She giggled, and swayed a little, just to tease him. "Like this?" she said.

"Bella," he said solemnly, "you can just be quiet for a moment, if you will."

She bit her lip but could not suppress a smile.

"Fold your arms," he said, and she did so.

Then—oh, Father, this is the very best part!—Julian took his sword from its scabbard and held it aloft for a moment, commanding the crowd's attention. When all was quiet, he lowered it, flat side down, and touched her lightly upon the shoulder, three times. And in a booming voice, he declaimed: "Isabel, daughter of Martin and Beatrice Smith of the village of Castle Down, in the name of God and of all the saints in heaven, I hereby make thee a knight."

Now what think you, Father? Was that not a good story?

# 14

# WILL

Mother came to get us at the forge. Father was repairing a broken scythe, and I was working the bellows. We both thought it strange to see her there. She had tasks of her own to attend to and would not normally interrupt us at ours. I wondered if something might have happened to Margaret.

"Martin!" she said, breathing hard. I think she had run all the way. "A page has come, in royal livery. He brought a message from Prince Julian!"

"Is that so?" Father said, pulling the scythe out of the fire, though he had just that minute put it in and it was not nearly hot enough yet to work upon the anvil.

"Yes! He says Julian is on his way here and will arrive soon—and he bid me fetch you home, and Will, too, for he wishes to speak to all of us together!"

Father put down the scythe and took off his leather apron, and I did the same. I could tell he thought the matter as curious as I did. Julian's visits had ever been private and without any pomp or ceremony. Though we were glad to see him again after so many years, the manner of his summons had made us wary. Perhaps he had some grave matter to announce. Had the king died? Had war broken out again?

As we neared the cottage, I saw that Margaret was waiting in the yard, staring up the road at the great cloud of dust in the distance. Julian was traveling with many men and horses, then.

"Has he called the whole village out?" I asked, still trying to make sense of it—though I saw no sign that our neighbors were leaving their work and waiting for the prince to address them.

"No," Margaret said. "The boy called us by name—he said for Mother to 'go and fetch Martin and Will.' And then he rode back up the road." I knitted my brows. Margaret shrugged. We waited.

As they drew closer, we saw that Julian had indeed brought many knights with him, and they were all dressed in full armor, their attendants carrying banners. They were very splendid indeed. I wondered if perhaps he was planning a tournament. But if so, what had that to do with us?

Soon they were near enough that I could tell which one was Julian—for he did not have his helmet on—and I broke into a broad grin. He had ever been such a small boy, and slight. How he had mourned over it, too, saying he wished he could be a big oaf like me! And now here he was, all grown up, taller by two handbreadths at least, with broad shoulders and a nice little beard—the very picture of a manly prince!

I did not know if I ought to wave or call to him, with those other knights about, and so I just stood there and smiled.

Julian reined in his horse and dismounted. While the knights watched, he came forward and embraced us, one by one—saying our names and beaming with joy. It was all so very *odd*. Only Mother kept her composure.

"My dear Julian," she said, "how we have missed you! Dare we hope you have come back to live again at Castle Down?"

An old nurse has certain privileges, and Mother knew it.

"Only for a time," he said. "I have important business here, and then I must return to the palace. My brother, the king, has need of me."

"We have heard somewhat of that," Father said.

"Then perhaps you have also heard of the Worthy Knight and the miraculous events that averted a war."

"All the world knows of it," Father said.

"Would you like to meet him?" How his smile grew then!

"Meet . . . the Worthy Knight?" said Margaret, her eyes wide.

"The very same." He gestured to one of his companions, who rode forward a little way and nodded in our direction. I saw that his armor was all white, just as we had heard it was, and upon his surcoat was the image of a plumed helmet ringed with fire. He was small for a knight, but he looked very grand indeed.

"Beatrice, Martin, Will, Margaret—I present to you Sir . . . Isabel!"

Then off came the helmet! And such laughter from the other knights at our astonishment! I was never so confused in all my days!

"She *would* come and show off her new armor," Julian said, laughing, "and could not be persuaded to wait even one more day."

She had to be helped from her horse. Indeed, she could not even walk unaided.

"Child," Father said, steadying her with his strong arms, "you are injured! What has happened to you—and why are you dressed so? What does this all mean?"

"But Julian has *told* you, Father—I am a knight!"

"Bella, you are having fun with us!"

"No, Father, not at all! Ask Julian—it was he who knighted me. And isn't it grand?"

"Julian?" Mother said.

The prince nodded and addressed her with great solemnity.

"I think you will like this story," he said. "Our little Bella here traveled all the way to Brutanna, to warn me of the attack. When I could not stop the battle, and all seemed lost, the Spirit of God came upon this wee daughter of yours, and caused her to ride like a fiery angel through the lines of soldiers. She brought two armies to their knees. Now what think you of that, dear Beatrice? Was it not worthy of a knighting?"

Mother began to weep and nearly crushed poor Bella in her embrace.

"I just *had* to come and tell you right away," Bella said. "The king has not only granted me a title, but lands and a great estate, as well—and I want you to come and live there, and help me manage it."

"Bella, you look as if you are about to faint dead away," I said, for indeed she did look very pale. "Margaret, run and fetch her a stool."

"It is only the excitement," Bella said as we helped her sit down, "and the long ride."

By then most of our neighbors had come out of their houses to see what was afoot. Bella waved and smiled at familiar faces. "It is so good to be back," she said.

"Do you suppose Lady Margaret could act as squire and help Sir Isabel out of her armor?" Julian said. "And do not give me that look, Bella. Your leg is nowhere near healed, and the wounds in your shoulder were treated for weeks with goat dung and sour milk. It is a miracle you are alive. I have indulged you thus far with this grand entrance; you can indulge *me* by taking off the armor, which weighs more than you do, and then coming back out here for a few moments more — after which I suggest we feed you a good meal and put you to bed."

"Hear how he orders me about!" Bella said. "And me the greatest lady in the land!"

I lifted her up, then, and carried her into the cottage.

"Blacksmith!" I heard Julian say with a laugh. "I believe he could carry her *horse* in there, too, if it were needed!" Then to us: "Take your time! We shall wait!"

We all worked at unbuckling her armor, so far as modesty allowed. Then Father and I went back outside while the women dressed her in Mother's Sunday gown. How small and thin she looked as they helped her back outside and seated her upon the stool.

"Now," said Julian, taking a deep breath and

looking first at Father, then at Mother. "Bella has made her proposal—and I hope you will accept it. Her estate is very large and will require much attention and sound management. She would be very grateful for your help.

"But she also wishes to thank you in this way for your great kindness to her. And truly, you deserve it. You set her upon the right path and taught her all that is good. It is to your credit that she grew up to be the honorable and courageous lady she is—and so you have done the kingdom a service also, and it is fitting that you should share in her good fortune."

"Oh, won't you come, *please*?" said Bella. "Auntie Maud will be there—you remember her—and my old grandfather, also, and my stepsister Alice! Oh, Margaret, you will like her so much, and both of you shall have such splendid dowries! And Will, there will be horses and a park to hunt in, and Mother, there will be cooks and chamber maids to wait upon you—"

"Bella," Father interrupted her then, "we have no need of such things, nor would we know what to do with them." In the pause that followed, we looked at one another in silent council. Then, having agreed just as silently, Father spoke for us all: "We know naught of managing estates, Bella—great or small—but we know the land right enough. If you want our help, such as it be, then it is yours. And if the duke will give us leave, we will go with you gladly."

She tried to rise to her feet, then, so as to embrace us, but she lost her balance and almost fell, her arms waving wildly and a foolish look upon her face. I caught her and set her back upon the stool. She might have become the greatest lady in the land, but she was still the same old Bella.

"Good!" said Julian. "Then it is decided, and I am well pleased. Bella, I think you would do best to keep your seat for now, so as not to break anything else."

"Yes, Your Majesty," she said, not so very respectfully.

"Now, there remains only one more question to ask, and then we shall take Sir Isabel up to Castle Down, where she can rest."

Father nodded, waiting.

"Good Martin," he said, "I speak to you now as Bella's father—"

"Oh, no, Prince Julian—in truth she is not mine. Perhaps you did not know of it, for you left here before—"

"I know *all* about Sir Edward of Burning Wood and care nothing for him at all. It is *your* daughter of whom I would speak. You always called her your little princess. Would you permit me to make her one in earnest?"

Bella gasped, and I forgot myself and laughed out loud at the wonder of it.

"You will consult with her first, of course," Julian

said. "To see if she is willing."

Father was ever a shy man and not inclined to show much feeling, but a smile crept upon his lips, and he could scarce control it.

"Daughter," he said, "what think you of this offer?"

"Might I be married here at the village church, among my friends and the people I love?"

"Yes," said Julian. "I would have it no other way."

"Might I wear my armor to the wedding?" she asked.

"No," said Julian.

"He will not allow the armor," Father said.

"I would like to wear my glass slippers, then—for they were made for a wedding and are strong enough to dance in. Only I fear I lost them in the forest."

"Know you aught of these slippers?" Father asked, turning back to Julian.

"It is most fortunate," said the prince, "that since you are inclined to leave precious things lying about in the woods, you have *me* to come along afterward and find them for you. I have your slippers and you shall dance in them."

Father turned back to Isabel.

"Tell him," she said, "that I know not how to dance!"

"Tell her," said Julian, "that once she has recovered,

we shall find someone to teach her."

"Well, then, daughter? If he teaches you to dance—will you have him?"

Bella grinned. "Ought I to consider it for a while, do you think? Keep him guessing?"

"I don't believe you would fool anybody," Father said. "You have loved him all your life. Are you willing, Bella?"

"I am," she said.